cabana the big

cabana the big

Ron Charach

Copyright © Ron Charach, 2016

All rights reserved. No part of this publication may be reproduced, stored in a retrieval system, or transmitted, in any form or by any means, without prior permission of the publisher or, in the case of photocopying or other reprographic copying, a licence from Access Copyright, the Canadian Copyright Licensing Agency. www.accesscopyright.ca, info@accesscopyright.ca

Tightrope Books
#207-2 College Street,
Toronto Ontario, Canada M5G 1K3
tightropebooks.com
bookinfo@tightropebooks.com

EDITOR: Deanna Janovski
COVER DESIGN: David Jang
LAYOUT DESIGN: David Jang

Produced with the assistance of the Canada Council for the Arts and the Ontario Arts Council.

Library and Archives Canada Cataloguing in Publication

Charach, Ron, author
    Cabana the big / Ron Charach.

ISBN 978-1-988040-12-7 (paperback)

    I. Title.

PS8555.H39834C33 2016   C813'.54   C2016-905346-6

For Eugene and Paul

The language marches in step with the executioners.
Therefore we must get a new language.
Tomas Tranströmer
from "Night Duty," translated by Robin Fulton

What did one ball say to the other?
Why are we hangin'?—Slim did all the shootin'!

Ah'll be yore narratuh.

Awl ya need t'know about "Slim" Reggie Canuck is that Ah was the developuh who got Harold Galloway his summuh place north of Wyomin'—on the Canuck side of the borduh—long before he left his wife and decided to use his pluto-cratic influence to build a biosphere to save the sorry asses of hyoo-manity. Stole the i-dea from Biosphere 2, jest north of Tucson, Arid-zona.

It stahrted as a CELSS. In Galloway-speak it was a Controlled Ecological Life Support System. Not that Galloway knew much about life. But he was the only show in town jest before the second big bang.

When Ah declined to drop the capital lettuhs from mah name and to ride with the big eight—like Tarantino, galloway jest *had* to do *The Magnificent Seven* one better—he ask'd me to tag along as his aman-yoo-ensis, galloway-speak fer the word *slave*. There was nothin' left t'do but drop my "unaccented Canadian English"—as he called it—and adopt his new shiftin' Southern stylebook to the hilt, mebbe put a little Canuck spin on things now 'n then.

Sure Ah could talk like galloway an' use commas an' subordinate clauses an' try to turn this sow's ear of a story into a silk scrotum—but all the propuh English in the world an' all the propuh Mandarin couldn't save the world as it once was—

So Ah tapped into galloway's listenin' posts and room bugs 'n wrote everythin' down—and whatever Ah couldn't di-vine, Ah sur-mised—lettin' the characters speak fer themselves, in their own post-apocalyptic way.

At fuhst, Ah had about as much freedom to tell things mah own way as Siri did—galloway's slave before all the electronics went kerflooey—but gradually like cabana Ah did things my own way. Ad-herin' to galloway's style manual means mah punk-tuation ain't worth shit—but then agin it never were. What Ah will do is let you in on what passed fer normal aroun' here—though no one knows what goes on behind closed doors—be they bed-rooms, board-rooms or domed survival bunkers.

Ah'll be weavin' in and out of this like Muhammad Ali—jest don't expect me to wave at you whenever Ah re-appear or take mah leave.

Not that galloway would author-ize the honest account that follows.

He warn'd me: —Keep it simple, Slim Reggie! Don't you bury my epic in rhetorical flourishes. So, permit me to *bullet* you the main points that posterity need remember:

- Billionaire genius harold galloway saved what was left of the world.
- He created cabana to keep things hopping, then used divide-and-conquer strategies to contain him *and* his seven familiars.
- Dr. Henry Morganstern was thoroughly corrupted, *and* his kin were either neutered or neutralized.
- There were detractors, but they were amply and humanely medicated. The women on the left and John Gideon on the right may have grumbled, but in the end, were powerless to oppose the genius harold galloway.

In other wuhds, they wuz *helpless, helpless, he-ell-pless...*

You wish—harold galloway—you wish...

If there is a reader somewhere out there ya might want to turn off yore sell-ular de-vices—if such things still exist—and pull the condom of tolerance snug up over yer face as we try t'git thru mah oh-so-rhetorical version o' this sordid tale.

Yup, *cabana the big* as told by "Slim" Reggie Canuck, without the benefit of Otto-Korrect.

If thangs get a mite narsty here and there—either blame cabana or blame galloway his makuh. Jest don't shoot the messenguh. We had plenty o' that goin' on already.

As the froggies used t'put it: *Ne tirez pas sur le pianiste. Sur le pénis* is more lak it.

APPARITIONS

cabana the big

As cabana the big saunters in you notice from a distance that one of his legs is a mite shorter than the other, the effect bein' like a bullock in purple-dyed leather lone-stars whose one heel strikes terrazzo a good two seconds before the other. But you don't jest sidle on up and say —Whajja do—forgit to slide in one of yer gait-breakers? 'Cause if you did he'd just smile as if to say *suck rocks*, maybe roll his metallic eyes around at you for an hour 'til you wished you were dead. Save the orthotics jokes for the afterlife.

Any room cabana enters becomes a situation room. In his off-time he gits off on rollin' oil drums at the once mighty cariboo, every now and then scorin' on a stag with seven-pointed antlers. The noble beasts are all Dreamworks overstock just like the eighteen exotic Plasticine dino-saurs that grace this dimly lit biosphere.

cabana likes to chuck oil cans at little birdies and other endangered species—now and then scorin' a direct hit on a nestful of spotted owl eggs. He's proud of jest about everythin' he does and most of all he's proud of his name. It was in a steamy shower room that someone first had the gall to look down from cabana's furnace-like glare. And the sight of *it* hangin' there like a section of Keystone XL jest an inch off the ground was enough to tag "the big" right on after his name.

Call him jest plain *cabana* if you want to. But you mightn't really want to. 'Cause if you do he jest smiles as if to ask, *What's that rhyme with?* You do some mind-work damn quick, likely wince and answer *banana*. Whereupon he rips off his gator belt, the one that's *species intactus*, and whips you with it repeatedly 'til you have welts like scarification lines. Either that or he might jest stand there: roll around his casino eyes at you 'til you wished you were deader than dead. With cabana's victims such a state is more than possible.

Respectfully, in what by now has become ritual, the townfolk whether chosen ones or mutants ask sheepishly: —Excuse us sir but is *that* your *gun?*

But if you get in good with him—play it cool and through a narrow lens—you might one day sit right next to him for a minute or two in Carla's saloon. Sort of turn to him real easy and flash a cusp or two—never show cabana more teeth than you have to—and chance a quick *Howdy cab.*

But keep it to a minimum. Or cabana will get *his* up.

And that one-eyed trouser snake is jest what you might refer to as "firmware." It makes even harold galloway's grand central power cable look like a string o' spaghettini.

For hardware cab tilts towards a Glock 19 or 22 or a Royal Blue Python .357 Magnum, sometimes an FN Five-seven with armor-piercin' capacity, a SWAT team fav'rite—Colt .45's bein' more than a little passé. Shit, they all was machined in the USA, even the ones with the Krautiest names: *Sturm-Ruger-Mini-14, Mini-Breivik, Steyr-Mannlicher HS .50, Heckler & Koch, Glock, Glock Glock... Sig Sauer, Sieg Sauer!* Names 'at would make Uncle Addie's little toothbrush moustache twitch upwards in a satisfied smile. What side really *did* win that war?

cab's partial to flesh-rippin' hollow-point bullets and X-tended ammunition clips—fun fare of the former Texas/Arizona gun shows or scofflaws down ole Tacomah Washington way, purveyors to John Allen Muhammad and his Beltway sidekick Boyd Lee Malvo. Didn't *they* ring a few bells...

Hell, when you're hung the way cabana is, it'd be pointless to apply for a CHL, or a Concealed Handgun License as galloway would call it. *Yas-sir! cabana is free and open carry at its full-frontal best.*

Like that ole bumper sticker: Gawd, Gats, and Guts. Keep What's Left of America Free.

Too bad what's left ain't worth writin' home about. Least not in capital lettuhs...

cabana the big de-mythologized

In fact he is a real man, with a heart that beats and a navel that does nothin'. Sometimes he lazes around at Carla's just starin' at himself in the plastic-ivy framed mirror like pre-Governator Arnold, rollin' aroun' his eyes until even he feels hand-held-camera sick.

And there is a good deal more to him than a mere foot of flesh-toned tubin'. There are also two huge Britannica globes gone hairy with pulsin' dorsal veins 'n arteries that swell to every beat of his magnificent pace—threatenin' to ignite the very air he displaces. And there is also a certain—class. Like the swirl on a calligraphy *W*. His is the authority of walkin' quietly while carryin' a big stick. cabana is *there*; he is *together*—of a *piece*. Like one of those Mongolian arrowheads that whistles as it flies thru the air, makin' everyone duck to both sides.

Moves like a cross between Michael Jackson and an Abrams tank. And when cab goes by he *swings*.

carla's saloon

Carla loosens the x-lacin' on her Frisco dress, givin' cowpokes a peek with each deeply drawn breath. You can only make out shadows, but when Carla pushes, the silken teddy moves up and down softly enough to get you stiffenin' to her whereabouts and the potential for fresh milk in season.

She is lithe and catlike, tall for a woman—moves with a skater's stroke when you've tipped back a few whiskeys, curves around corners, pelvis in sight long before the rest of her arrives, moldin' the surroundin' scenery to the mood of her indigo dress. Gunmen and hired hands watch her out the sides of their eyes; her sly motions tickle like them hesitatin' bubbles that leap through the room-lit haze of freshly poured sham-paigne.

Around closin' time, when the mutant bus-girl Lucy mops the broken glass and yawns once or twice so Carla will see jest how tired she is and let her take her life in her hands sneakin' home on the back streets, Carla awakens to full form. She insinuates up to the tallest table, where only the big ones dare sit playin' stud, five card and four—kings and queens flashin' by so frequent you'd think the deck had nothin' *but* face cards—every now and then an ace flyin' by, pullin' a grin across one of *their* faces even as it darkens the eyes of the others. By now all the young married mutants have been hauled home, and the boys and girls of the town are in dreamland. galloway's best-in-show townies are slavin' away in some underground machine shop, keepin' the life-blood flowin' to his brightly number'd oh-so-silent generators.

No man of minor mettle would dare walk the streets with the sounds of flyin' cards cuttin' the night like a deck. Carla alone is the womanhood sittin' it out with the meanest and the best, long after the midnight valve has closed on the town and the townies in their beddy-byes and nightie-nights.

As she perches on the glass tabletop eyein' their tremolo playin' hands, each of them secretly watches for shadows. The pyramid V always peeks into view when she sets herself down, that Guccione V between her firm settlin' thighs and jest beneath ground-cover, a dusky grassy knoll you don't dare to think on. Oh, the white-pantied V that no mincin' little ridin'-up nothin'-o-a-thong c'n approximate.

Carla clicks her pink tongue at a snake-eyed young one 'til he starts playin' recklessly, awaitin' a response. She smiles, with those tunnel-end pupils and only a long gold hatpin piercin' her broo-nette pulled-back hair to warn: here is a woman with class and bite. If you show her teeth, make it your ivory best. Only gifts from the range-flats she'll look at are diamonds—no enamel or glass or bits of glintin' quartz need apply. And *please*—no zirconium.

Since no one has diamonds or gold any more she moves freely around them, sittin' only on a whim on that caramel quim so unthinkably out of reach that you'd need t'be an ack-ack-ac'tuary to fully reckon its worth. cabana-like guts to drop trou and go in after it.

galloway

Sweet 'n Low galloway. Splenda. galloway of the Microsoft soul. Like the other Donald—Rumsfeld—who made his fortune hockin' NutraSweet and Metamucil, galloway catapulted into the Pentagon's graces by learnin' how to de-hydrate pretty nearly anythin' ya might need when sittin' out an unclear war in a bunker. Then graduated all the way up to DARPA where he made himself as indispensable as a fume hood.

Would have to stand on tiptoes to kiss a rat's ass. So tight he squeaks when he walks. How many clichés would it take to put him down so right he'd stay down—clichés drippin' off the mealy mouths of those low enough to consort with him. But even clichés are too good for this silver-spoon'd slop bucket. *Inter urinas et faeces nascimur*, said St. Augie. Well, he must have had ole harold galloway in mind. *Pfffft... pssss...kerplonk!*

galloway pathetic at five ten. Too crooked to fit a urinal and couldn't go anyway with a real man standin' beside him. *Why do they design urinals in little intimate duos? Who was the closet dweeb that dreamed up that one?* frets galloway. Nerdy li'l shoulders in suit-jacket paddin', *Deltoides absconditi*. Every minute of his life he's playin' Careers: ask him a favor and oh yeah he'll do it sure he will—but he'll carefully enter it in a ledger so detailed it'd make a loan officer cream his pinstriped trousies.

Deals in charts and graphs for one reason: so every deed in his life will have alternate import, secondary gain—his life one big Columbus voyage with the sole destination of the elusive ass-hole of progress, puckerin' for a kiss. *Now, that's fulsome.* Lucky for galloway there are those around who adore the feelin' of wet lips on their posteriors. It's the thing he does best—when push comes to shove.

    galloway makes a capital investment in Carla's saloon. Four hundred shares, at a greasy five a share. Slides out an endangered-species wallet and dusts off his Harris tweed suit, worn to establish an abrasive image under a well-blocked bowler. Bastard son o' Bat Masterson.

    C'n neither shoot straight *nor* ride. In-tention tremuh an' knock-knees. Canters down the street on the only horse with enough death in him to be safe—a reguler *annuity* of a hoss. Steps over the many cables leadin' to his precious generators an' gently leaps the grand central cable like it were part of a steeplechase for Shetland ponies.

    Reinin' he tips his hat at the ladies—or what's left of them—tuneless merriment spurtin' from his puckered lips. About as convincin' as a foreskin in a flower-show—Harper, Toews an' Nicholson crashin' a women's book club. Or make thet Harper, his undertaker Blaney an' squeeze-faced Petey MacKay of the sixty-five un-con-tested F-35s. Shee-yit—they was all sent packin' by Kid Tru-doo—banished by his sunny ways.

ma rosemary

What can you say after you've stared for an hour at the crack'd spiny back of a blue-grey lizard smolderin' in a sun-gutted wadi like the last reptilian life-form to escape bein' Gucci'd? When you've rubbed your burnin' hands in the bit of wet sand you finally clawed to the surface, tryin' to keep your lips from bakin' in the brain-drillin' global warmerin' heat?

Well then—what d'ya say to some ice-cold cider?

And if that's wayyy beyond just a thank you—what words are good enough to describe the li'l ole mid-life honey who brews it jest fer you?

When you drag your ass back into town on your dribblin' Appaloosa, clutchin' its straw-thick mane—no longer able to look up into that ozoneless glare outside the dome—you can always tie up at ma rosemary's, and she'll welcome you and yer hoss, waterin' the latter with a jug or two of Crystal Springs then helpin' you peel yer buckskins before you stumble into a shower-stall then a feather bed while she takes yer temperature *in three places* as you fret and rub yore eyes like a snot-nosed brat. Then listen as she pours a pint full of the world's best cider, freshly squeezed—make that freshly thawed—New Zealand orange pippin without so much as a hint of Alar, all mulled in cinnamon 'n clove spices, with re-constituted "fresh" bread to slosh around in it.

And you don't have to say thanks 'cause ma don't take thanks anyhoo but jest sort o' shrugs 'em off and beams: —There's plenty more where *that* came from, cowboy, now you just catch some beddy-bye. She'll even send you off with a little rub 'n tug fer those who ask po-litely, nudge you gently into delta-wave slumber.

Course, only the big ones dare come by. Who else would show up with the likes of cabana or big ned skulkin' about? Each of 'em grins as she com-pliments his great looks or walks by with a pan of hot epsom water for his saddle-butt or *Gawd*-awful smellin' feet—and all the while *she* smells like fresh-cut hay, her round far side o' middle-aged form jest as springy. Woolen shawl a-swervin'—spotless even at its frayed old edges. The big ones take to talkin' like little boys at a birthday about buyin' her presents for all 'at she's done. But the would-be birthday girl just colors and makes them take back those silly sagebrush wreaths and rattler necklaces. She tells 'em to give Carla more business instead—to keep up their whiskey, their gamblin' and their jest-fer-sport gunfights and all the other boys-'ll-be-boys thangs that ma knows her big ones need for distraction.

About the only time she lectures—ma does—is when one of them's been wounded fer real—most often by cabana since he never-ever loses. She'll cry as she holds a com-press to a slashed arm or leg or a split upper lip.

—O for sem a' ma's cider, grits big ned somewhere, wipin' the sweat off his brow with a crusty ole forearm. His pointy teeth take on a smile as he considers ma rosemary smilin' back at him even though she's a good five miles away. The only other livin' thing that'll smile back at ned is cabana who does it frequently on a dare. Course, dust-covered rattlers on the range will show him two drippin' fangs apiece and one day will get him—if cabana don't first.

Maybe one'll surprise him this very night as he struggles with those range-beans with the sand mixed in 'em that crunches like glass, an' farts up a Mel Brooks sandstorm gettin' flashbacks of fresh bread and cider—and ma, *da good ole painted lady 'at makes 'em.*

louise

Louise lies belly-down on the last bit of lawn left anywhere, runnin' her slender fingers through the lost memory, whimperin'. She strains and pulls up little handfuls thrown high into the air as she laughs and catches her breath then looks around, then does it right over again without even wonderin' why. Post-apocalyptically.

She walks back home while the dim light still shines, sad whenever she looks into the lemony orange sky, brushin' wisps of hair fallin' over her watery eyes. All she wants is to have someone who understands and who cares. What girl of fifteen could do otherwise?

Her sweater around her waist in a bow that she ties and unties, lyin' still in the shadowy sundown of the small deserted farmhouse where she lives almost alone—out of view of the dull glass dome in the distance from which only fearsome riders would venture. And she looks up from the middle o' nowhere—like the girl in *Christina's World*.

jamie

But all is not innocent or still. Louise has a little boy and he belongs to her. The story of how it was—when Louise was grabbed and pushed apart and hurt while she fell into a merciful swoon—is too much a nightmare to recall. Just to say that she had carried a little boy inside her and brought him out with the help of a mercy visit from a handsome mid-life midwife known only as ma.

She nurses him with still-pointy breasts and she washes him.

She guards her little one—readin' him stories of a happier time as he dozes in sleep natural as a seagull on a dump-site—before leavin' for the silence of the wild lawns of astro-turf outback. Always sure to return before he awakens—to a mornin' song, a warm hug and honey kiss.

She lives with her candy boy. And no one knows but ma rosemary and a CEO on a horse who brings what they need every now and then—no one else feels these sad peaceful days of lazy rollin' on the last remainin' bit of furry green; no one else knows of Jamie's frolickin' in cotton dreams, the two of them in cradles rocked by sickly listin' westerly winds.

POWERS THAT BE

time slots—cabana's vow

This mornin' cabana's patrollin' the streets at 6:45 a.m., for a reason that can be best summed up in one simple word: Friday.

It's like this: first thing in the mornin' is prime moseyin' time. Not a soul in town is up except for ma rosemary and Carla, who have to prepare for their daily services during the wee hours. Or maybe galloway's off somewhere, dozin' by one of his closed-circuit monitors.

Now you might guesstimate that any of the big ones energetic enough to be up at 7:00 a.m. after a wild night of drinkin' and gamblin' would have free reign to stop in for a cider or a health check at ma's or a few pints and an eyeful at Carla's. But there'd be a catch to any one of 'em takin' advantage of so sought-after a privilege: each of 'em is after it. And no two of 'em can walk a street at the same time without takin' at least one or two potshots at t'other. The temptation of two hung-over, ornery men walkin' a deserted street in the middle of a desert town would make for showdowns *a priori*—if not sooner.

So the big ones—and there are eight prowlin' these parts—must rely on the help of galloway's mock-Crackberry to divvy up the early-mornin' shifts—not for love of order or schedules but as a measure o' pure survival.

On Mondays fallin' on even dates cabana patrols the old main street and heads on up to Carla's or ma's. On Mondays-odd, it's the turn of no one other than fat-ass jake—strictly WWF material. (World Wrasslin' Federation *not* World Wildlife Fund—ya enviro-dweeb!) Tuesdays are shared by billy, even, and bloody willy, odd; bloody willy has an arrangement that if he can't make it he's stood in for by his younger brother bloody willy too, whom nobody's ever met. Wednesdays go to big ned—alternatin' with a cousin of the big eight, a late in-duck-tee, the former medic henry morgan. While on Thursdays it's the trapper dan show. trapper gets Thursdays odd *and* even 'cause he's too loco to figure out the difference. In fack there's been talk lately about re-vokin' his early mohnin' privileges, on accoun' o' he squanders the morn without botherin' to visit Carla *or* ma. He fritters away his prime time settin' grizzly bear traps all over Main Street that a specially ass-igned townsman named Parkinson has to spend half of Thursday afternoons removin'.

It's worth ten seconds (no more) to explain the unique personality of trapper dan, t'do a genetic-dynamic formulation of this redoubtable gent. trapper is constantly approachin' folks and darin' 'em to bean him on the head—claimin' not without jestification that his head is a mite-shade harder than granite. His personality is testimony to just how many people have taken up the invite. Even a classy dude like cabana took the time to bop that old eggshell of trapper's with a meat tenderizin' mallet offered expressly for that purpose.

So even though it don't make sense to let trapper dan stalk imaginary grizzlies while the rest of the big ones hanker after bare-naked ladies—he hangs on to Thursdays odd *and* even and will go on keepin' them 'til cabana or henry morgan or a notice from galloway at head office decides it's worth the time and effort to exterminate that brain-dead varmint.

Fridays-odd go to slick black amos barton—also new to the big set—the silver-spurred dandy of the group—gated comm-unities and racial profilin' be damned. He's the last-but-not-back-seated number eight of the big ones.

Well that might cover the handlin' of the mornin' times—'cept once they were divvied up there were still times left over. Namely: Fridays-even, Saturdays-odd and even and Sundays-odd and even.

Sundays-odd and even went out o' commission suddenly when Carla took to decidin' to sleep in late that day—fer her beauty 'n all. Saturday nights bein' particularly hectic and requirin' ample recovery time. Fridays-even were snatched up neatly in a coup by cabana amid an uproar that lasted five suspense-filled seconds—'til cab reached down for his 'gator belt with the ammo clips. Saturday-odd fell to big ned, which left only Saturdays-even. Fer a change of pace Saturdays-even were awarded to cabana.

Worth notin' that should big ned ever con-fuse an odd with an even he'd meet square-on with cabana on the latter's day. Which is why ned's backside (shaved slick for the purpose) is tattooed with a calendar—December through May, June and Ju-ly on each hammy buttock and August through November runnin' down the back o' each leg. Carla sometimes calls him My Calendar Boy—though The Illustrated Man 'd be more like it.

With all that explained it's not too difficult picturin' cabana sidlin' kind o' vertically up the old main street on a sun-fried Friday with not a soul astir in the entire town 'ceptin' Carla who happens t'be the proprietary pie of the very place where he is headin'.

With steely deliberation he moves his left leg then his right, hinges creakin' slowly, coolly, pins in his shoulders makin' faint warnin' noises—like a saloon sign slappin' in a dust storm—that give others plenny o' time to va-moose. The pins stem from an ole gunfight with big ned durin' which cabana had both arms blown clear off—only to have them affixed right back on with a couple o' ma's trusty bobby pins. To this day, any time cabana sus-stains a flesh wound there, you can spot tiny flecks o' dandruff that once nestled in that good little woman's hair lyin' scattered along ditches o' dermis.

cabana, lookin' askance, half-expects to get a flash of ned down the way though there's nothin' but sagebrush blowin' down Main Street and no sign o' townsfolk save a broken-down wagon some poor dude had t'leave behind once he realized what day it was and checked the fine print o' his life insurance for a clause that might limit the amount payable.

Straight before cabana's geodesic gaze appears this flashy new sign—a sign with a difference—an ad-dendum:

CARLA'S SALOON—Take Yore Spurs Off*
*big eight Ex-clooded

With a little smile kind o' inchin' up on him, cabana gives his buckskins a brush, secretes the smallest amount of WD-40 on his forehead for some shine, squeezes his vice-grip hands—an' mounts the steps to that curvaceous cutie. Pushes open the wooden saloon doors bitquicker t'avoid them swingin' straight back on him—*goddamn* them doors—and is bathed in the soft light o' a buck-antler-*cum*-crystal chandelier hangin' over tabletops of buffed cherry wood. As Carla primes the beer taps, her nervous helper Lucy frets away at the back, sneakin' a toke of aromatic freeze-dried BC bud, courtesy of harold galloway.

Now if'n he were jest any young cowpoke he'd a' simply parked a Hummer with antelope-catcher, hauled out his cell phone and while on a call simply said *Mohnin'* to Carla and her young dys-morph assistant. Maybe order a pint while fiddlin' with his portfolio on a hand-held devious, maybe an I-me-me-my-Phone or a And-droid or a nostalgic Canuck Crackberry—and only after he is good an' finished, exchange a few words with the comely young lady or text-massage her, sext her or jest send her a poke or a tweet.

But cabana says sweet diddly. Jest cringes his inner lips—tight enough so you'd need a pair o' Bushnells or an Owl restaurant light to spot the motion. From the outside he looks like he was hacked out o' stone with a chisel or like some huge slab o' con-glomerate careened off the side of a rockface. Calm and craggy: he blows dust off his sleeve onto the bar an' tightens his widely rangin' arm t'reveal flexors an' extensors of Schwarzenegger variety—then grips a beer glass that Carla slides his way nice an' smooth-like. Aimin' for the ashtray, he spits into it a thin sliver of metal. Then in-spects Carla as she sits there lookin' near as wily as wary. And all this time naughts the word. Just sittin' there sippin' alcohol—incorporatin' it into his limbic centers with the efficiency of Japanese blottin' paper.

Lucy knows better than to look up—never while cabana is savorin' a silence. After fifteen minutes of such, Carla dares to stretch her curvy back along the wall of pioneer log, and up through her ribless waist of pure sinew and frisky-puppies chest she eases a whisper: —Ain't ya heard, cab?

Nothin'. Not a movement. Not a flicker of *ak-ak-ack*-knowledgment. Carla waits—her slender foot tremblin' just a tad below the bar rail as cabana takes to strokin' the longer edge of his beer glass.

Little Lucy petrified. Watchin' clouds in her coffee. Sees cabana all stony and unflinchin' and recalls how he once stood jest the way he's standin' now: then in a second a furnace flash as he hauled out his silverware and pumped twenty bullets into a townie who'd asked in the wrong way: —Excuse me, sir, but is this seat taken? Evidently, tragic'lly, it *was*.

But a tiny crease starts across his face, two creases, movin' downward into definitive lines. Lucy drippin' sweat, tryin' her best not t'look up. Wants to scream *HELP!* when the cringe turns into a pointed grin. An' cabana slowly answers

with a slow turnin' of his turret—in a kind of a no.

Once cabana lets you live you might as well keep talkin'—havin' by-passed the point of maximum danger, though Lucy's bite-plate is saggin' as her boss forges on: —galloway...

No change in cabana's flintlocked face.

—galloway's done terminated my lease; wants to turn the saloon into—an' she mimics the runt who sounds out his every word, proper as a Muskoka-cottage Canadian—a "profit-making ventyoor."

More silence.

She goes on: —So I says to him, hell with you, ya Ivy-League-intellectual, Wall-Street-apologizin' loser. I ain' goin' to up my prices none—even if you do so happen t'provide the nourishment an' call y'self mah uncle. I bin handlin' service 'round here two long years now an' I see the big eight 'at stop by here as *my* boys, same way's ma rosemary.

cabana may have nodded his head a mite at the mention o' ma.

—An' he answers back, galloway does: —Please refrain from comparing yourself to ma. It's dis-respectful. Just like that, he answers me. So I tells him—uncle harold—er, galloway: —You *keep* yore stinkin' money.

—But he won't take no fer an ans'er. He says —If you don't co-operate, I shall have to revoke your license or perhaps travel to the nearest neighboring "town" where there just might be a C-for-Certified Marshall, posse in tow, or remnants o' the National Guard to make sure that the eight and their little server-girl go the way of all other flesh. And wouldn't I like to save him from goin' to that kind of trouble—knowin' full well that he's docketin' his time like a partner-track corp'rate litigat'r even as we speak?

No movement from cabana. Carla pressin' a dishtowel to her décolletage.

—So finally I says to him: —Jest what do you think *cabana* might say if'n he knew that some fed'ral marsh-all and his pissy little posse or a dozen neo-Nazi guards might be payin' us a visit? To which he answers—and I kid you not: —cabana, *shmabana*—

cabana veers. A twelve-ton cat swervin' like an Abrams as Lucy faints—nose dippin' into her coffee and bubblin' like a small toy boat goin' down in a bathtub full o' Soaky. Flips a piece o' silver out o' his pocket, throws it clear over his shoulder so's it lands smack-*dab* in the center of an ashtray—and he's outta there—legs bowed with rhino intent, with the word *galloway* breakin' out in veins across his temples and his sculpted lips a bloodless white.

big ned is summoned

Two hours later that same Friday big ned wakes up. The early awakenin' may be without precedent, but it is not without cause. For big ned had been dreamin' about a little insect takin' a walk along the inside of his skull, makin' tiny stompin' noises as it wriggled 'round his hemispheres with imp-yoonity—bleatin' indistinguishable insect gibberish as it scratched along his semi-circular canals. This enraged big ned since any intruder into his lair was likely smart as he was, the cave dust notwithstandin'.

His eyes open wide. He can tell they are open 'cause suddenly he can see—all-be-it filmy at first. Things generally look fa-miliar: The splash o' puke on the mattress from last night's bender, the urine stains—*goddamn* that asparagus!—the red mud on the doormat—the sour remains o' milk spilt from the cracked bowl on the yellow washstand. Even the straw tickin' on the cave floor jest lies there—spider webs full o' abandoned li'l legs—like a tab-low straight out o' *Better Caves and Gardens*.

Except for that confounded natterin'. Instead of the muffled noise of the man-made waterfall gushin' outside the boulder door, ya have these crazy li'l insect steps.

big ned cusses himself for startin' dreams he cain't finish. Tells the insect to bugger off and is about to stuff his head into the thickest of the spiderwebs—sort o' try to off-load that insect to one of those chubby but merciful-quiet spiders—when suddenly the noises draw together, into a distinct: —*big ned big ned, please, are you in there!?*

—Goddam' insec' a-hole—up'n callin' me lak thet! ned spits stringily—the nerve of an in-vertebrate actually callin' his name. *Why, dem insec's so dumb dey can' even wrat dey own names.*

Volcanically: —Dis insec'll take special gettin' rid of! And pullin' a torch off the cave wall sconce he is about to smoke the insect out o' his head when he hears a slightly more distinct —*It's me*—*harold galloway*!

—Dunno any bug ba thet name—'cept fer *one*.

ned shoves aside the boulder at the mouth of his cave to reveal galloway tip-tip-tappin' at one of the cave walls with slender white signet-ringed fingers. galloway backs up at the sight of ned standin' there naked as noon and then freezes. The insect noises cease. After lookin' him up and down and debatin' whether or not to crush him—ned settles for sweepin' the air with his huge paw in a kind of Entrée-Euro-weenie gesture. After all, hadn't galloway set him up in this plush little cave suite in the first place? big ned does a belly-flop on his mattress all damp with moanin'—mutterin' obscenities into a lake of drool slowly eatin' its way thru the pillow.

Briefin' him: galloway in a bind. big ned, won't you help? big ned aloof. Fast asleep on the mattress. galloway cautiously nudgin' the corpulence with one of his one-per-center CEO tasseled shoes and ned showin' signs of listenin'—wiry ear hairs bristlin'.

—Five thousand dollars are yours, ned, if you save me from someone Out There who's trying to get me. An ass-sociate of yours who's getting too big for his britches. Five grand of the real ones, ned—nothing hot about these.

Last payment ned received from galloway was a mite more devoid of watermarks than bills oughta be. ned up again nearly awake.

—Are you with me, ned? Five G-notes, just to hide out and ambush him. Plug him *from the back*, ned. Is there any other way?

big ned gurglin' into the mattress—the drool spot slowly spreadin'.

Obviously *with* galloway all the way.

In foul or sunny weather...

Through the mattress goes a great-big muffled roar, as galloway reaches for his wallet. —In fifties, ned, or would hundreds do? Perhaps thousand-dollar bills would be preferable—two now, three later? Balance paid on completion? But big ned is asleep again—couldn't make it through the word *preferable*—especially this early in the mohnin'. Sleepin' sound as the late Guv'nor Perry used t'do on the night befo' a lethal injection.

galloway lookin' down at the dozy ned with a feelin' of dis-may tempered with putrefaction. Decides that what is lackin' is a moe-tivator. Goods and services always better than money with the likes of... More concrete. Somethin' even big ned might go for. Elevate him from lazy lout to motivated moron.

galloway leans his shoulder-padded back over ned's hair-filled Victrola o' an ear—holdin' his breath as he does and whispers in high fidelity about a very young thing that ned *just might* take a shine to. A girl on the *virge* of young womanhood who's illegally campin' out on one of galloway's many abandoned rural propitties—usin' water that galloway pays for.

—She's no more than fifteen, ned—just about the age you like them, untouched and in full flower, like an amaryllis, and just hankering for a bit of your sweet action—that is, if it's given the way only you know how to give it, ned—that is real hard, harder than the bunker-bustin' missiles our late president laid on the former Saudi royals, ned, so hard no blurry-eyed debutante or interne could help but be wowed, soak clear through her cheerleader freshettes—you with me, ned?

And ned's ear takes to twitchin' and there's twitchin' goin' on further south—as a puddle mucilages onto the mattress—time bein' the only thing ned don't waste when he's excited. Rollin' over on a mammoth haunch he stares up at galloway's perfect white crowns. A great wide bloody-gummed grin sweeps across his Bluto-channelin' face.

—She dun got no pappy er mammy t'kill fust?

—No, ned. That's the sheer beauty of it.

Scoutmaster enthusiasm takes the place of the business-like air that usually trusses his face as he sweats on.

—You just have to head straight out and get her—except of course, only I know *exactly* where she is, and if you tried looking for her all-by-your-lonesome on my far-flung holdings, you'd have this entire territory to cover, now wouldn't you? And you'd be glowing like a bulb from the all the rads.

ned unimpressed. Couldn't make it through the word *territor—*. galloway senses a lack of sentience—rises to the occasion: —The only cowpoke that's good enough for this hungry little sex-starved kitten is yourself, ned. She wouldn't let the likes of cabana or trapper dan within twenty-five feet of her fleecy pussy.

ned grinnin' at the mention of cabana's name alongside that of the mangy trapper.

—We can count on you, then, ned? As he flashes him the best of his we're-with-you-all-the-way-son grins.

big ned tortoises over onto his other side, stretchin' his crusty corps across the mattress—then flips onto his back an' guffaws at the ceilin'. Stops. Twists his bearded mug towards galloway as his right hand scoops an enormous black peacemaker out from under the mattress.

galloway shits.

But big ned just takes to fondlin' the gun on his stomach, its long curved scrimshaw handle nearly worn bald from overuse—his eyes tight as the anuses of two waterskiers—yawnin' and smilin' as once again he surrenders to the oceanic feelin' of that most loneliness-relievin' of all words: *Puuussy!*

Shaken but recoverin' galloway backs away from the cave. Sets up a fancy fibre-glass MEC tent he brought along on the back of his surrey and camps out—awaitin' ned's rousin' time—whensoever that may be.

Picks a pen from the neat row in his pocket pro-tector, and on monogrammed stationery writes a letter to some foster agency in a let's-pretend Washington—arrangin' to have some family pick up little Jamie, the baby he knows young Louise is hidin' and who he's already begun to think of—half-affectionately—as The Kid. All this bein' *pro forma*: for the sake of fillin' out forms.

Recalls a quote from Alexander King: —That gentlemen prefer blondes is due to the fact that, apparently, pale hair, delicate skin and an infantile expression represent the very apex of frailty which every man longs to violate. Couldn't have said it better myself.

Composes an ad, for the town paper, *his* paper—a funeral notice for a young man named cabana who at the untimely age of twenty human years was felled by a bullet through the back—in an industrial accident:

Contributions may be made to the Town Safety Council.
Accidents Don't Just Happen. They Are Caused.

And, lickin' his finger, he sets to writin' a second piece—a combined news story/obit—for a tragically abandoned youngster named Louise. Just in case she gets silly and tries to resist big ned—the eminently resistible ned. But decides to cross out the phrase *repeatedly raped and mutilated* because anyone readin' such a phrase might suspect that the man 'at wrote it were more than a townie local editor—and somethin' of an Ivy Leaguer—in short, one of the elite: A Serious Man.

big ned's dream

big ned alone in pitch black with nuthin' visible on any side 'cept fer a tiny point o' light somewheres in the distance up ahead. He stomps down tryin' t'reach it—when *AYEEEE!* his ears ring like sirens an' his head swells—the pain too sharp t'bear without grindin' the teeth. From all over the black rebound sharp vibrations from the sound of a single footstep strikin' iron beneath him.

The whole cave must be an iron cylinder 'cause it reverbs every noise ten times louder into a hollow roar that tears at the eardrums—raisin' blood in the middle ear.

Too terrified t'move, he jest sits there starin' fearfully at that far-off teasin' dot of white. Beggin' fer someone to help though he can't even whimper 'cause even a whisper would come back as a roar—a thousand roars that would deafen and sicken to the point o' dry heaves.

So he squats in bless'd silence—knowin' he's a goner.

And when his hairy hand moves t'wipe sweat from his face, he feels a beard like the wire on a barbecue brush and above it his face too is hard 'n cold as iron—every bit as hard as that iron floor sweatin' rivulets of thin brown rust.

Waitin' and waitin' out a dream that lasts forever. 'Til sudden and true he feels the iron floor drop open on its hinges—leavin' him magickly suspended smack-dab above a apparition now uncovered and about t'awaken. It's a sweet and milky-soft kind of girl—the same kind of sweet young innocent thang that's always been a-feared o' him.

An' he fears the young girl will let out a scream soon as she makes out his bulbous jet-black silhouette hangin' over her.

But she opens her dreamy eyes to look him over an' surveys his hairy domains an' moves *t'wards* him. An' *her* hands don't cause that deaf'nin' noise. She touches him with love even though his frozen mask of face has no way to show jest how powerful-bad he wants her.

She rises like the flame on a candle towards him, leanin' over t'kiss him, and melts the iron straight off him—turnin' the floor beneath 'em both into an ivory-white polar bear rug straight out of a Hef mansion shoot. All she's wearin' is a downy-soft teddy over skin as glistenin' as silk.

An' he feels his-self changin' back to flesh again—hot breathin' animal flesh with the spirit returnin'. Yet there's one part, one ever-so-lucky atavistic 'n centrally located part that *stays* metal, safeguardin' the sacred form of long metal shaft—a missile out of its silo—leapin' up a good fifteen degrees off his belly midway 'tween his furry thighs. Bold as the casin' of an ICBM or a Trident or the latest special creation o' the good eggheads at DARPA—it refuses t'melt into the surroundin' eiderdown, but remains vintage ramrod like that sacred obelisk every young thing itches fer and wants to slide around on like a red-helmeted firegirl as it slashes in and out—in and out—now slicin' through, piercin' an' chawin' divots as it re-tracks with an eye and a mind all its own like a colossal drill minin' the gen'rous ore and sacred spoor o' raw love.

An' his li'l green-eyed teen dotes on his glistenin' metal kisses, his beefallo lips, an' guides the vanadium slashin' between her whoozy young legs, eatin' at her insides in a mixture o' pleasure an' pain she wouldn't have any other way: —*O stay hard there cowpoke!* She's as satisfied as ten Japanese businessmen in a cum circle around a naked geisha carryin' out a life-endin' *seppuku* as they jerk off into her ripped entrails on the floor of a specialized porn site—all court'sy of CGI—*that's* how satisfied as she throws back her goldenrod hair and screams —ned you cum-sweatin' loverboy—you Silver Bullet Man, you Marlboro Man, you First-Man-on-the-Moon Man, you *Don't-Tread-on-Me* Man! Her innocence rubbin' along him like a polishin' o' emory cloth as she takes it in—eatin' his iron head—his Mr. Big Tree of Love as' th' lights take to flickerin' up a storm.

THAT'S HOW I WANT IT, NED. YOU BE SOFT WITH ME IN THE OPEN—BUT WHEN WE'RE ALONE YOU BE HARD NED. RAISE ME WITH YOUR LEVER NED LET ME BE YOUR WRAPPER NED YOUR LOVE-CARTRIDGE. CARTRIDGE FOR YOUR BULLET NED YOUR WICKED SILVER BULLET NED—YOUR SERIAL KILLER BULLET NED—YOU'RE JOHN WAYNE GACY AND BERNARDO, ERIC HARRIS, ADAM LANZA, DYLANN STORM ROOF, MIKE CAR-NEAL AND ELLIOT RODGER ALL WRAPPED INTO ONE!

An' he cries. An' in-hales deep. An' knows full well that he loves and is loved for what he is and must be. And that it's right because she wants it and needs it and will not run away...

And will not run away...and will not run away...ned stands back up pourin' sweat. Panics at the sight of iron all around again. Screams, NOOOOO!!

But then stops 'cause there's no echoes now—jest the old familiar darkness of the cave. Eyes accommodate as horror-heads dissolve in the retinal film.

The dream has stopped. *In-outus interruptus*—galloway havin' turned down his cranked-up Eagles o' Death Metal album *and* the strobes. ned don't remember his dreams: dey's uswally denged fecken styoopid anyhoo an' fyoo a dem evah-done-was *wuth* memberin'. But senses this one's diff'rent. Somethin' 'bout a young girl. Recallin' galloway's promise of a li'l one 'at *needs* It and that he wants so bad To Give It To. An' knows he's already well slid down the greased path t'true luv—

Licks his tongue out a mite an' sort o' rolls his eyes a bit—imitatin' cabana—plungin' his hands through his underwear for a bit o' reassurance—vowin' t'give it good to that girl that'll soon be his. An' lies there smilin' through mornin', long past the hour he usually gits up to stare back at any upstart sun thet tries to jump-start another day.

And he almost takes t'thinkin'. Lookin' up at the cave roof an' picturin' his-self hangin' from there, bein' lowered down onto her liquid sunshine—picturin' how much he needs that girl but how he don't fancy messin' with cabana to git her, which might only lead t'doublin' or triplin' his navel. Tryin' t'figure a way that he c'n pry that girl from galloway without helpin' the latter complete the assignment at hand. Squeezin' his puddin' brains for whatever last bit o' mileage they'll give him.

a bit of anaesthetic

henry morgan eyes his wife Claire as she prepares for bed, and she catches him out the side of her eye—getting ready.

—Put your hand somewhere else for God's sake, she scolds, bra straps dropping to her sides, twin cups falling to the floor. She snaps up the flannel nightshirt her mother once bought her, the one with the tiny Laura Ashley print that he finds about as sexy as a tea cozy.

—You're just jealous, he says dryly.

—Look, she says, turning halfway from him as, under cover, she eases out of her panties that fit more loosely than they used to. —It's bad enough I have to tolerate your stares whenever I get ready for bed, do I have to watch you doing *that*?

—Does it really bother you? You should be flattered.

—You're impossible. She storms into the living room, her backside forming tight little pitcher's mounds, expressing themselves even thru that sex-effacing garment. The vertical frown of her makes him want to spank her scarlet.

—O come on hon, he calls after her, though what he really thinks is *silly cunt*.

—I'm not your piece of entertainment—and there's no point in our getting back together 'til you find me half as exciting as you find yourself, and we all know who-else out there...

—Whoa now Claire, whoa. It's one thing to accuse me of hangin' out with the guys too much, it's another to go accusin' me of cheatin' on you. I mean, golf widow is one thing, spurned woman another...

—There's more than one way to abandon your wife. And by the way, it's just not natural for a man to pull on penises the way you do.

—My own.

—No matter; a penis is a penis is a penis.

—Gertrude Stein, right? *How would she have known?*

—There was a time when you would recite Gertrude Stein.

—Only to myself, though.

—Why keep coming back, henry?

—Feedback, Claire. A man needs feedback, even from his awfully-wedded wife. A little head-to-head.

—If that's what you need, go down to your ma rosemary; she's got mirrors up on every wall and the ceilings too, I hear, and plenty of sweet small talk to spare. And isn't your old buddy weird harold an Ivy Leaguer? He can give you plenty of head-to-head...

—But only *you* give me *head*.

She breaks into angry sobs. He marches into the kitchen and looks around for sandwich fixin's. He considers putting his still-half-erect between two slices of bread and springing the combo on her with —*I reckon you don't like it when I play with my food, either. Take a bite out of this.* Though she just might take him up on it.

A good joke or a prank could sometimes wrench her from her funk. Mr. Goodwrench.

He pours himself a tall glass of lemonade and sits down. Nearly jumping as his bare ass strikes the cold vinyl chair. Soon she'll come join him. He can almost hear the silence in the next room as she plans what to say next, the ever-predictable Claire.

Once he had thought it might be tolerable to live with a woman who enjoyed thumbing through *People* and *US* and *Cosmo*, who preferred the plebs newspaper to the yuppy one. For lofty matters you always had your guy-friends from the old schools or buddies in the Boys' Book Club. She ambles into the kitchen trying not to look sexy, a losing proposition when her back is turned and she is that much easier to objectify. As she passes he thinks about how wrong he'd been to plunge into a relationship while still in medical school. With someone who folded under pressure more readily than he did.

She's abandoned the flannel gown. A change of heart? Of hormones? Plenty of *those* in galloway's cocktails. And now wears one of his denim shirts, and nothing else—has tied the bottom few buttons' worth of it into a bow, which is fine by him, 'cause it leaves just a tad of her bottom peeping through, making her long long legs even longer, covering over her upper haunches that, even with the weight loss, are more pocked with cellulite than either of them dare notice. He motions her to come sit on his bare lap. But she shakes her head: first finish our talk.

As if this were a *dialogue*. Hardly fair criticism, of course, since galloway's meds don't exactly enhance her mental powers. Quite the jack-of-all-trades, that galloway.

He wants to tell her that talking to her is a soliloquy. Instead he grabs her by the shirt—*his* shirt—and pulls her up and over his lap.

—*Leggo!* she yelps, slippers flying off as she kicks for his face, hands twisted behind her back inside his powerful grip; the shirt slides down over her like a lasso, and he wrenches the bow so he can control her from behind. Her fairly firm if mottled ass is squirming, but her thigh and leg muscles strain 'til he is near the point of firing. With his free hand he snatches the ice-cube tray from the table, easing up on the shirt, giving her a bit more line, and smashes out some cubes, scooping a handful and holding them between her buttocks and slit 'til she squeals and nearly tears free with her thrashing. He's like a curved ruler and in a second pulls her onto him, the two of them dropping to the kitchen floor in a heap of limbs; in a second she is around him like a pair of plyers, and he twists through sluice gates greased with the juices of a good fight. And all the while she mutters —*Bastard! Bastard!*

When it's over, she walks slightly bow-legged from the bathroom and asks him for a back-rub.

—You like my surprise?

—Couldn't you tell? But this is getting rough. We're not as young as we once were, she says, rubbing her aching wrists. —Why does everything have to be from behind with you?

He has the sickening sense that she'll soon start overeating again. Then restricting what she takes in for days on end. The way they clash these days only fuels such behavior.

When she falls asleep against him, murmuring *henry, my henry*, he bets that soon she'll take to sobbing in her sleep again. Luckily he won't stay for long, won't have to hear it. He watches her innocent sleep, surveys the more-than-she-really-was grace of her long neck, her small breasts—flattened still more by the ravages of gravity—floating up slowly with her breathing, his own sinewy lever of an arm wrapped snug and dark around her waist like a smooth bough bent by an expert maker of canoes. So Ondaatje…

She might yet tell him: —You were way too rough.

To which he'd snicker and defend himself: —Hadn't I applied a bit of local first?

A joke only a former medical receptionist—*his* medical receptionist—could go for.

henry morgan to the rescue

Two mornings later, because it's decision time for henry, Claire is at her worst.

—That little thing we did the other day, I hope you don't consider that making love...

—Least we made *somethin'*. You seemed to like it well enough. You even said so.

—Look, henry morgan, I did not marry you to have you get your head blown off your shoulders.

—Get back to your back-issue chick magazines and housekeepin' reveries. And I'll ride with the eight, handicap and all. That's a choice I made.

—Spare me that "big ones" crap again: the choice you made; you'd think I was never part of the choices you made...

—That was then, this is now. Now and again you still figure in.

—How *big* of you. And when your brain comes oozing down your nostrils, I'll be left alone in this godforsaken place...

—...in a godforsaken universe...but if that's all you're worried about, goodbye, Claire, 'cause Ah'm no thee-ologian—

—henry wait, for the love of God, wait!

—You and your God.

—You were my handsome young doctor, you wore silk ties...

—Yeah, galloway ties. I remember too. There were plenty o' ties back then. One fer every shade o' shirt.

—You were *somebody*. You *helped* people, and I did everything to look after you—even followed you out here. Where a woman can't leave her home without risking the crossfire, where we would've had to keep our kids indoors all the time—had we been able to conceive. I had a brave handsome husband with a clever mind, who could converse instead of drink, who drank fine wine instead of rot-gut...

—And who catered to the medical needs of galloway and his executive cronies, don't forget that, my little chronicler. Ah, Manhattan, Old Greenwich—nothin' but the best out-o-pocket could pay...

—Stop it, henry. You always put too much on that selling-out excuse; it's your easy out.

—No, you always ignore it. As if I was some kind of pinstriped saint or something. Goddamn it, Claire, where do you think the money we floated our lives on came from—or are you able to wonder about such things? It came from exorbitant fees and speeded-up services in galloway's "privatized" clinics—why, I robbed near as many people as cabana ever shot, though I confess I was never as slick a robber as galloway.

—Why compare yourself to *galloway*?

—You see through him too. It's just that you don't let it, or anything else, shake you to the core. Oh, the power of a woman, to take life one day at a time, one pharmaceutical dose at a time.

—That's not fair! How can you, a grown man, walk out on your wife and medical career just to strap a hunk of steel to your waist and traipse around like a simpleton—then condemn me for accepting help from the only man in town who's kept up his education, well, aside from that yes-man Doc Halverson. I *need* these injections; you make it sound like there's a choice.

—Oh, I forgot: *I'm* the only one with choices around here—

—You spend your life at that sly old bag ma rosemary's—who's got nothing better to do than cut slice-n-bake cookies for a bunch of...

—You've said it already—a bunch of simpletons.

—That's right, *blamed* simpletons.

—Can it, Claire. I've heard this before. You know nothing about ma rosemary or about the big picture around here.

—I've tried to get through to that woman. You'd think she'd have the decency to return one of my notes. *Damn, I miss that iPhone!* Then there's that little hooker, Carla.

—Look, Claire, you just take your shots—as you say, you're not a well woman. If they're what you need to keep goin'... Comfort yourself with the knowledge that we have *real good reasons* for puttin' up with this B-movie set-up. There ain't no other place to be.

—That's how you always end it: nowhere else to be. Yet you refuse to let us make more of the time we have left. You just ride with those overgrown desert rats. Programmed to do nothing but murder and maim, like some first-person shooter video, and you fancy yourself worthwhile, just because you're ...

—Direct, Claire. Ah'm direct.

—Go ahead, *keep faking it!* Maybe that's all you did as a doctor too—fake it. Else you wouldn't have quit. Believe me, henry, you've given up a lot more than just the capital letters in your name.

Hmmm, nicely put.

But he answers: —Oh, so I was a fake doctor too? Yet you always play up what I *used* to be.

—I was a young love-struck fool.

—You still are. At least the fool part.

—Asshole.

—Don't you mean *prick*?

—Fine, then—prick. *Doctor* Prick.

—Flattery will get you nowhere.

—Flattery! That's all it is, isn't it? You're flattered to know you can still hang on to your pri—but wait henry, don't just walk out—where will you be!...

—Why, with my peer group, the seven mental midgets, or whatever you want to call the big eight. Forgive me, but I think even if it *were* still an option, I'd take a pass on Freedom-55, loungin' with you on a long purposeless ocean cruise. At least with the eight it's—*unpredictable... minute to minute...*

—You should have taken up golf, henry. You'd have had all the obstacle courses you needed—*and* a chance at a hole in one...

Hmm, she must be reading more. Ironic, to be educating herself this late in the game. But then, galloway stockpiled quite a collection of ebooks and remaindered books, "works on paper," he would laugh.

—You know what I really miss, henry—really, really miss?

—What?

—My iPhone. I keep reaching for it like some kind of, er, lost arm or something.

Yeah, you'd like to be in on my every move, wouldn't you...

—Yeah, it's like yore phantom limb...

—Pardon?

—Never mind. Try not to even think about that kind of thing. All them apps and all the bells and whistles of that cyber-crap... Littly cyber-birdie whistlin' at you whenever you got an incomin' text. Bots that organized your day and even kept the pest calls at bay. Don't even think of it.

—I miss my Facebook, my friends and all their likes, the timeline, posting photos... I miss streaming music so much! I miss Twitter, Instagram, Snapchat I miss... Ohhhh!... It's so awful to have it all gone!!

—You had cyber-friends. One step up from imaginary friends...

—That's not fair!

—This'll all jest drive you to distraction... I'd best be goin'. Just remember: there are *reasons*.

—I'm turning the deadbolt, so don't think you can come back any time you want to. And don't forget to keep your cell on...

—Yeah, sure. You want to keep moonin' over what's long dead an' gone, then just go right ahead. Suit y'rself...

—Henry?

—I don't answer to that name no more, ma'am.

—henry?
—What?
—Do you love me?
—Not now. Sometimes...
—Do you hate me?
—Damn right. You're hard to live a lie with.
—Where you off to? You going to fight?
—More likely to watch one.
—Who this time?
—cabana—he's out lookin' for galloway.
—Those two can't fight, I mean...
—Right. The new world order won't allow it. But I reckon galloway will pro-cure himself some help and hide out in his bunker 'til things are set right again.
—Who will he get?
—Rumor has it that the lucky number's been drawn by big ned.
—big ned fight cabana? I thought they were friends.
—Yeah, regular co-leagues.
Chuckles all 'round.
—They'll fight anything 'at moves, those two. After all, they're also di-rect. Don't talk much. Think less. Anything more I say might give it all away. Bye, Claire.
—I can't hear you—wait!
—Bye.
—Whose side will you fight on?
—I dunno. I reckon the winner's.

an uneventful day. carla closes up —and opens up

big ned doesn't get up this Friday; his subconscious jest keeps him sleepin' an' sleepin' an' never even tries to raise his hairy ass. He is 1) too hungry for the girl to up an' tell galloway a plain NFW (no feckin' way), but he is 2) terrified of the *thought* o' havin' to elude cabana's radar face long enough to plug that patickular gent in his patickular back. So he sleeps and goes on sleepin'—jest gettin' up every hour or so for a minute, lookin' out around the rim of the boulder blockin' the entrance to his cave t'see it's still light out there. Murmuring *shee-yit* an' hittin' the sack again. When he finally gets up t'seein' it *is* dark, he jest tells himself: *Well then it's night ain't it? Reason enough to reach closure an' hit the sack again for the Big Eight—hours, that is.*

galloway for his part just sits outside the cave waitin' with the determination of a credit-card co-llection agency. He owns the land that the cave is on and had it wired electric'lly in th'event he'd need to coax a bit of help out of dumbbell ned through the use of a little hands-on procedure. He lies on his roll-away futon-on-wheels—goin' over his accounts under the e-lectric lights that run off his portable generator, keepin' business affairs purrin' smoothly through the vast wire grid that runs under his sizable holdings. All in all—it only takes patience since ned will get up sooner or later.

Back in town nobody—but *Noooo-body*—left their houses that day—what with cabana prowlin' the deserted streets with the blood risin' through his tumescent flesh 'til he looked like an atomic sugar beet sulkin' an' shootin' at whatever moved in his blindin'ly rapid inimitable way. cabana didn't care to register where in hell galloway might be 'cause while he'd gladly stoop low enough to pump galloway ful o' lead, he would never set his uninsulated foot on that yellow-livered smart-ass's home ground. 'Sides he always got dizzy—some sort of phenomenon akin to the jammin' of his early warnin' system—whenever he left the downtown dome for the outer terrain. He sensed the whole-damn ground on galloway's acreage was jest bristlin' with frequencies 'at only a dog could hear—that contained sub-liminal messages only a dog of a man could take notice of.

As for henry morgan, he'd gone down earlier—just a few blocks shy of the downtown—to come an' join whoever was fightin' when he heard dozens of gunshots reportin' an' realized they was all comin' from the self-same semi-automatic. You could always tell cabana's gunshots 'cause they had a *Gawd*-awful strong smell to them—like a combo of beer farts and cordite—as fishy as the "right to carry" at a Diamondbacks game or a Tucson parkin'-lot exercise in out-door democracy.

cabana was sendin' out tracers for galloway so that galloway would more than likely keep his self scarce—and with all them bullets sidewindin' around there was no sense hangin' out anywhere near Carla's, where a man could get into some body-piercin' mighty quick.

So henry took off to ma's on the outermost skirts of town—where she applied a washcloth to his forehead (best thing for stavin' off the ole hemi-crania) an' gave him a few pints o' cider—scoldin' him for dawdlin' so long with that dim and ungrateful wife o' his who spent all her time dwellin' on the past or chattin' with townies 'til she started to act 'n even sound like one. An' why didn't he come 'round to visit more often? You're nothin' like the rest o' the eight, henry dar-lin'—et cet'ra. ma had four out o' seven all sprawled about her livin' room—drinkin' cider or eatin' hot bread, belchin' 'n fartin' up a *Blazin' Saddles* storm an' braggin' about roadie movies they'd seen in galloway's "media room." Else they were jest lazin' about in giniral, mebbe waitin' for a hot bath in a lion's claw metal tub with an inflatable shell-cushion an' a few dribs o' health-food-store lavender oil. The only big ones missin' from this I-dyllic scene were cabana, big ned and trapper dan.

But dan soon joined them. He'd gone into the downtown area, which consisted mainly o' video arcades with Nintendo and PlayStation terminals since galloway redone it. The trapper missed out on the noise emanatin' from cabana's trailblazer on accoun' a he was tone-deaf. He'd been draggin' along his huge bear trap—thinkin' o' nothin' 'cept fer those great-big hairy paws that'd soon step into it—when all of a sudden cabana caught sight o' him roundin' the proverbial bend and shot a volley o' shots his way kind o' spellin' out the word *va-moose* in the dust.

The trapper vacated the area mighty quick and jest made do with settin' up his sole remainin' trap in the residential area. When he was through, he lay around in the garden in back o' ma's for a while, tonguin' away for cutworms an' then chawin' on 'em—whatta guy. But ma spied him out back and pulled him in by his mangy ear an' forced him t'eat some of her fresh-baked zucchini confection instead—made from the finest freeze-dried zucchini, the stuff growin' outside bein' purely for show or for townies to eat since they already glowed in the dark. The trapper took his cake on the back porch 'cause the other big ones wouldn't a enjoyed theirs anywhere near him—what with them cutworms stickin' in his teeth an' wrigglin' in his muddy beard so much you'd never think they was Bulk Barn gummy-worms.

Not a soul came to visit Carla's all day an' night. Even cabana never done took a moment's rest as shots erupted from his take-this-personally Ruger-Mini once his AR Bushmaster had run out o' rounds. Carla decided to close up shop. The bullet-proof awnings were already down, so all she had to do was bolt the steel door from the inside, send Lucy the townie home, turn out the lights, an' go out the back way down one of the steel-roofed catwalks galloway had de-signed as safe passages home for his van-guard o' coolies.

On the back door which she deadbolted, she put up the sign "CLOTHES'D FO' TH' NIGHT." Once it had read "CLOSED" but big ned corrected her on the spellin'—pointin' out quite correckly that when it was lock-up time folks grab their *clothes* from off the metal coat-racks an' leave. So ya oughta spell it *clothes'd*.

She made her way down the pitch-black "laneway" tunnel—damp an' metallic and lit every now and then by a million points o' halogen light, a kind o' faux indoor firmament—while bullets whizzed 'round and ricocheted through the relatively real night outside these protected con-fines. She winded and turned through tunnel after tunnel towards the part of the outskirts 'at was in the opposite di-rection from ma's—in other words galloway country—'tween the residential area and the desert proper. Once out o' the protective cylinder, she arrived at an open square where she could almost imagine real stars peepin' through the smudged glass of outermost dome. The center of that skydome was at least thirty stories straight up, an' she sighed at the thought of it. After a five-minute walk she arrived at her small studio "cottage," leased from uncle harold and made out o' the thickest logs in town—aluminum sidin', ack-tually, with a little frontier *trompe l'oeil* elevation.

She opened the door slow 'n careful and peeped around a bit nervously, flickin' on the lights real fast-like, startled by the reflection of her face in the mirrored wall—then just laughed at herself for bein' silly and threw her suede coat over the Italian leather sofa an' stretched her long slender arms in a drowsy yawn. She switched on the fireplace—artificial as galloway preferred 'em—'til it glowed an uneven orange-red then closed the rose linen drapes over the window with no view so her room was cozy as an oven-mitt. She touched the thick thermal windowpane just to feel how cold it was—these freezin' desert nights—and was thankful for the wondrous warmth of her bachelorette, even if it did have to double as a kitchen and bathroom as well.

Then she padded around a bit, makin' herself a bit o' tea, sittin' around in panties and bathrobe for a while, munchin' toast an' sippin' tea laced with just a hint o' warm brandy. She scratched 'tween her legs a bit. Where she'd been itchin' all day but didn't want to scratch in front o' Lucy who was a silly prude. An' when she finished eatin' she set the dishes in the stainless sink and walked back t'wards her sofa bed, pullin' it out an' dimmin' the rheostat 'til the light had a soft peachy glow. Feelin' warm an' protected, she slipped off her fur slippers and let her robe fall around her, peelin' out of her white panties an' givin' them just a little sniff t'see if they needed washin' and makin' a little crinkly-nose'd face when it was clear that they did. Naked 'cept for her bra, she strolled to the hamper then undid that too, lettin' her still-firm convexities wriggle up 'n down a bit as she gazed admirin'ly in the smoky floor-to-ceilin' mirror. So gentle and complacent she was—and completely unaware of galloway watchin' from behind the mirror less than half a yard away, his scrawny dick pulsin' in his hand. She strained 'n strained for a before-bed pee over the fancy rose-colored acrylic bidet uncle harold had installed for her. But nothin' came o' her efforts 'cept for a relievin' jet of air 'at galloway vowed he would never forget an' that he'd play back for henry morgan on more than one occasion—on one of them Blu-ray DVDs you could set on pause without blurrin' the picture.

Carla finished with the room lights and gave her mirror one last, well, not bad sort of smile then surrendered to a very deep sleep. Pullin' her covers up over her breasts, stretchin' out her long legs against the cool satin sheets, she buried her face in her pillow and hoped for a dream about another life, another world.

Her every bedtime move on video—all edited into one big long ongoin' sequence o' famil-iarity worthy of YouTube. *Just what would you like to see her do tonight?* he'd grin, his wide expanse of porcelain capped teeth pushin' apart his ratty ears. It came in handy when morgan got restive an' threatened to blow the masquerade.

While morgan looked around at the seediness o'ma's set-up—scarcely able t'believe he had stooped to watch a peep show courtesy of unca harold galloway.

louise closes up too

Louise had trouble sleepin' that same night even though she was far away from the town where folk lay quiverin', warm quilts pulled up over their ears as they waited for the gunshots to die down and for even cabana to go get himself some sleep.

She kept havin' bad dreams, a dizzy feelin'—she worried she might not always be well enough to care for her Jamie who slept soundly now. She leaned over his little wooden crib and kissed his eyes gently so as to not wake him. And as he slept on, she admired him, kissed him again feelin' silly for worryin', and wonderin' how life could ever end with such a beautiful young saplin' to live for.

She laughed, gently sat down on the edge of her lean-to bed, brought her legs up and curled into a little ball, just like Jamie sleepin' by her bedside, an' forgot about tomorrow easily.

accident

The weak light filters through the shears bathin' Mr. and Mrs. Parkinson's faces in a bronze anemic glow. Inside their eyelids the world is a dull red haze just strong enough to make them turn their backs to the window, press their faces in their pillows, and steal a few more dreams on a Sunday mornin'.

But noises outside drive home that it's time to git up and face the list of 1,001 still-to-do's and talk yerself into believin' for one more twelve-hour period that it's better to act like an adult than lie in bed with the "furnace" on and keep the cool outside air waitin'. Damn this man-made weather!

There's a ballyhoo goin' on outside among the few normal-enough, still-healthy kids left in the neighborhood, the rest havin' died off, there bein' no real hospital, just an infirmary and the new age of Survival of the Fittest—to quote harold galloway—havin' already dawned. The kids have struck up some kind o' ballgame or other—screamin' and jostlin' an' pushin' an' hollerin' 'til a body jest has to get up or his wife'll think she lost him in his sleep.

Parkinson's been charged by the town's peaceable citizens with dismantlin' the downtown bear traps—the kind that crazy loon trapper keeps settin' an' buryin' in sand or dry silk leaves. Parkinson himself has had a few close calls with those dust-camouflaged snappers and has ample cause to resent bein' the one appointed to find and disarm 'em—'specially when it's autumny cold an' still a bit dark in the mornin' an' just about anybody could step into one if he weren't A-one careful on Main Street.

The plan was for Parkinson to rise at eight fifteen—early enough t'be the very first man downtown since on Sunday just about everyone 'ceptin' the kids would sleep in. But here it is, goin' on half past ten. Sits by the kitchen table in pyjamas, puttin' on the kettle for a two-minute preparatory cup and throwin' on a pair o' pants over his sleepin' gear while he waits. Ma Parkinson is still far away from the world, choppin' wood in bed through clogg'd sinuses (bless her) and he watches her pass time in dreamland 'til his Paul Revere copper-bottom'd kettle gives a shrill whistle.

Relieved that it's "bright" out even if the desert sunlight diffuses into a faintly pissy color as it streams through the grimy glass of the main dome, he's glad to hear the kids are so happy on what to them, after all, is as sunny a day as they're ever gonna see.

They're deep in concentration playin' this "all-American" game that Reggie Canuck taught Henry Morganstern and that *he* taught the kids before he defected to the eight. A game kind of like the NFL 'cept more excitin' 'cause there are only *three* downs, which makes for a whole lot more passin'. Young Timmy McCarver throws a long spiral clear across the length of three front "lawns" and hits little Brent Donnelly for a seven-point major as they call it—*touchdown* bein' a bit too close to *countdown* or *meltdown* t'be a word galloway would want people usin'.

Little Brent lands with the ball in his hands, lettin' out the most excited scream the neighborhood has heard in a long while. Two plays later a newcomer to these minor leaguers—Gary Gordon—comes tearin' across the sidelines—which are really only sagebrush along the edges of the front yards—an' he runs a good five houses' worth before slidin' way outa bounds into a small pile of dusty leaves—lettin' out a diff'rent kind o' scream. His leg is on fire as some kind o' animal—fierce and iron-y—hauls him to and freezes him to his breath. The pit-bull of a thing's long metal teeth sink deeper in as his hands reach down t'try an' pull apart its jaws.

The harder he tries t'pry it apart the tighter it gits. The other kids come runnin' to see what the fuss is—screamin' an' cryin' at the sight o' little Gary wrigglin' and writhin' like a fish on a hook—his pant leg glowin' arterial red as the color drains from the rest o' him. One of the kids takes to bein' sick, another faints dead away, while a third runs t'git help—runnin' in an ellipt'cal path while lookin' down, way down, whenever he passes anythin' remotely like a bump on the ground. Soon every adult townie in the neighborhood's caught the difference between what's goin' on an' the enthusiasm a few minutes ago.

By the time Gary passes out, the kids have roused the adult world—such as it is—with the Donnelly boy poundin' on Parkinson's door so loud that Parkinson leaves his kettle on the boil without fussin' to rouse the missus. Soon every grown-up within a couple blocks o' the Accident is up 'cause the team captain is shoutin' for everyone t'come quick 'cause Gary's all caught up in a bear trap an' bleedin'.

An' Doc Halverson—who chased galloway's cocktail with some Scotch last night—brushes everyone to the side—even moves Mrs. Sheila Gordon, the boy's mother, off to one side and tells the father, Will Gordon, t'git that frantic lady away from there before she does more harm than good to her li'l boy lyin' there limp as a doll.

Doc was once a half-decent doctor even if he does work for galloway and got all his trainin' and equipment second-hand from henry morgan before the latter took out early re-tirement. But all he can do is stare at the mangled mess inside that bear trap while his hands reach for peroxide an' gauze and a li'l vial o' morphine in case the boy comes to again. An' he jest stares on accoun' o' he doesn't know how t'git the damn thing off—an' it's mighty clear that it's caught Gary high-up on the fe-moral artery, an' might soon jest bleed him t'death.

Halverson presses down on Gary's in-guinal region and yells for someone to find galloway and git him t'start an IV and hang some bags of that plasma galloway hoards like youth serum and stops short of askin' someone to find that crazy trapper who might know how t'git it off fast-like, since there don't seem t'be an in-tact release. But no one in their right mind'll go near ma rosemary's—which is where all the big ones'll be after their so-journ of the previous night. Of the bad lot, henry morgan's the only one with a wife he might have come home to, an' so Parkinson sends a townie out to the home of Claire an' henry morgan, cussin' in self-disgust because of all the people who ought to know how t'git these traps off... But then he's done such a good job these long months clearin' out these suckers, he's never really *needed* t'know.

Claire Morgan is up alright—housebound as usual and a bit confused-lookin', her hair all tousled, a home-rolled doob burnin' in her slender hand, though when she hears what's happened, she spits her husband's name like a curse.

Finally the trap has done its work an' the townfolk carry the boy to his parents' place with his top-shredded leg wrapped in a fresh towel tied up in a knot just above the mess an' with cold damp towels on his face and a little morphine in his blood and his very own teddy bear restin' spread-eagle on his chest. After he lies there a good ten minutes—an' Mrs. Gordon has been forced t'take a little morphine on top of her daily dose, and Mr. Gordon is offered a few swigs—a bear of a man named John Gideon—who was once the doctor's own aid, but who's restyled his self as a evangel'cal carpenter—gits up the stomach to take up the gnarled limb and wash it off an' bring it back into the house—pillar-white and floppy though it is—demandin' if there might be some way to sew it back on. But Doc Halverson takes on a sad look, almost as if rememberin' a time when there *had* been a way but jest answers —Throw it away somewhere far out o' reach, an' hides his innermost desire to jest sit down with the Gordons an' join them in their weepin' and adds —Wrap it good, John, so the rats don't get at it and do yore best to hide it away. And for God's sake, don't even consider *burying* it anywhere...*remember this soil*...

An' with his little boy flat out still oozin' blood an' bein' fed ice-chips an' blubberin' baby-talk his pappy hasn't heard from him in years, pharmacist William Gordon steps out into the dim mornin' glare and announces he is off to find that infernal trapper dan. To kill him. With half the town's menfolk sayin'—Don't be a fool. Gordon, who was the town druggist whenever galloway let him get into his stash, nearly forgets to take a gun and might have had to use his measurin', pill-countin' hands to do in the trapper—which would a'suited him jest fine and the i-rascible trapper even more. 'Course only the eight have real guns with ammo clips 'n all—though Bill Gordon managed to squirrel away his personal piece from his days livin' out in the dark nights of suburbia.

Someone from the town—some woman—had the sense t'clear the kids off the street—'cause by now even the mutants are gettin' into the act, wheelin' themselves to the doorways an' pokin' their heads from their Stryker-frames t'see what the commotion's about. The kids had t'be cleared so that Parkinson could check the rest of the residential area for any other nasties the trapper might've set in his infamous stupor.

An' someone else, a well-muscled blacksmith name o' Abrams, calls on John Gideon—who hadn't yet washed Gary Gordon's warm young blood off his hands—t'join him in gittin' up a mob of about twenty men still in serviceable health—for townies—to back Will Gordon.

John Gideon is not yet game. —The next child so trapped, he says, will also lose a limb. With those twin pillars of flesh we shall fashion a cross to hold up to anyone who trucks with the godless galloway.

You nuts? thinks Abrams, not waiting for an answer. —We have to do something now, today, *just this once...*

And figure this: the average age of this mob of retri-bution is forty-five; why, they's pretty well all circlin' fifty on one side or t'other. Everyone in the whole danged town 'cept for the be-nighted offspring and certain select members of the eight. Most folks might reckon the eight a whole lot younger if you could reckon 'em at all in human years. The only variations on these mono-themers are harold galloway—in his mid-fifties if he's a day—with henry morgan an' black amos not far behind. Course ma's age could not be estimated by anyone save the coldest-hearted of men and cabana can't count worth shit. The only age-mate of the younger eight in this-here town is Carla. Reason for takin' this informal census is the fact that this chorus-line of indignant forty-fivers looks like a businessmen's health club with a fitness program that's failin'. A mighty worked-up pack o' Boomers they be as they bite on their lower lips more desp'rate than enraged. After all—with galloway out surveyin' the range-land—there's no one t'tell them all to go straight home an' cool off. No elder anyone can accuse of havin' learned from advancin' years.

confrontation

Indian summer of a day. Mornin' coolness givin' way to hazy hot 'n humid under the dome. To hell with little bleedin' Gary says the far-off sun, splashin' dim yellow over everythin' like a basin of stale piss dumped from the window of a three-story roomin' house—damn them unreachable, uncleanable domes with the infinitesimal particulates that never seem to clear once they settle, rain or no.

As William Gordon heads down the main street t'wards the outskirts, he passes ten dozen dazed-lookin' people who know what happened to his son and who can only shrink down t' the size of their own sad horizon-lines. *Clomp clomp clomp.* Determined Will Gordon in an old pair o' motorcycle boots henry morgan outgrew by two sizes—galloway's moseyin' by-law preventin' townies from ownin' cowboy boots. Wild Bill Gordon peripatetic pharmacist—out to avenge the sins of the fathers with a thin ribbon o' townsfolk trailin' down a sidestreet in an effort to head him off before he reaches ma rosemary's.

And they do. Gordon rounds the corner of the ole livery's hitchin' posts t'find he's starin'—down the sandflats jest at the very edge o' the dome—at a crowd o' thirty or so allies, silent-starin' townsfolk with shovels 'n blades 'n antiquated garden rakes—no guns for townies, galloway's by-law on Accessible Media. Course—the black market bein' what it is—there's a piece or two that evaded galloway's inspection now pickin' up undershirt scent in the crowd.

They're awaitin' the word. To avenge a thin but springy child's leg that right now is gatherin' flies atop the old deserted annex—where John Gideon risked high radiation readin's to go an' toss it. Why yes, Gideon fairly did throw that parcel o' human flesh—bones an' all— mumblin' a prayer as he let fly one o' God's own pretty ones' once-tender flesh—hardly the first piece of kiddy sawed off in a mis-calculation, land-mines an' cluster bombs an' missiles launched from drones bein' what they are, and the former US o' A havin' been in no big hurry t'ban one bit of it.

The mob and Bill Gordon look straight-on at ma's where the only sign o' life is one curtain openin' jest a mite. At the side of the house are seven horses waterin' an' jostlin' each other for feed—with the only one missin' belongin' to big ned. But cabana's horse is there—to no one's good luck but his own—an' that stallion—or is it an androgenized mare?—is showin' its teeth an' wavin' its tail o' braided wire at the gatherin'—snortin' an' spittin' out the lesser oats, pawin' at the turf as if she c'n sense the impendin' action.

As the door to the house *flings open*.

An' standin' there is jest one man. An' it ain't big ned—'cause he ain't even there. And think a bit harder—'cause it sure ain't trapper dan, who the mob would want to fire at in somethin' approachin' unison with whatever pieces escaped the confiscation. And you best bet it ain't billy or jake or old henry m., not even black amos barton nor willy an' o' course it ain't ma—'cause she's busy makin' poultices for whosoever survives. It's cab. Standin' copper-eyed, prismatic'lly shootin' back the rays o' sunlight 'til the eyes of the townies start to smart an' make 'em consider the few comforts o' home.

The mob begins to shuffle some. That old familiar silence kills and you don't need your metaphors when cab's around 'cause he pretty much serves as his own com-parison. These shiverin' souls are brave enough—if paunchy in their midlives, though here and there's a blacksmith or carpenter with a bit o' ripple left grippin' at a jetblack hammer for good luck. A baker name o' Kelly with a reconditioned Colt .45 held straight out horizontal-like—pointin' cab's way albeit for some in-tension tremor. An' a livery man name o' Frank with a long whip an' a blue crowbar t'hurl if he gets a chance to. And Jones and McTavish an' Orest an' Schulberg the banker with their wives' tiny derringers held high in sweaty hands as they quietly in-tone th'original Latin. An' John Gideon that reborn Christian type who fancies himself a carpenter. And finally, William Gordon—counter and dispenser of pills—willin' to die here with nothin' more than hate curled inside his sweaty fatherly fist.

An' Gordon squeezes out some words—his moundy throat dry 'n tears startin' to form at the corners o' his eyes—so unaccustom'd to public dyin' are these pharmacists who fight other people's setbacks with labeled potions and photocopied 'structions. His raspy throat croaks out a tentative: —cabana…

Now why in hell did he up and say THAT? think about ten men.

An' Gordon squints straight ahead into the visage of that nouveau-legendary figure—an' he wants to go on 'cause he knows that the words that oughta follow go somethin' like: *Please stay out of this, cabana, we're only here for trapper dan—to stop this insane trap-laying once and for all. My own boy is dead, cab, I mean DEAD—and there's nothing that can ever bring him back.*

But cabana turns this father pre-cambrian, an' all those suck-cinct words he was fixin' t'say are aborted like hummin'birds that got stuck to a crazy-glue feeder—frozen like stalactites formin' in his grittin' enamel.

cab's foot takes to sort o' movin' slowly right—sideways as if he were drawin' a line between his authority and these-here ass-embled emotivists. He kicks a bit o' dirt—his hands near his spangled triangle, hoverin' over his shooters. Isosceles stance.

An' the mob's thinkin' *Why isn't Will Gordon sayin' somethin'* an' a couple o' men start to cock triggers—waitin' though for Gordon to call off cabana with a good ole-fashioned explanation.

Kyaaaaaaaaannnn!
Kee-yaaaaaaaaannnn! Keeyaaaaaaaaannnn!

ricochets cab's volley—lettin' fly—the hot lead meltin' in flight an' whizzin' an' buzzin'—makin' you wish there were still subway entrances to dive down as the mob disperses for its ko-llective life. An' cab's guns keep blazin', one firin' then t'other and t'other agin 'til there's thirty or more shots comin' from each barrel—an' shots goin' on even as he slides in another ammo clip— an' it's clearer than day that there's two sets o' semi's at work a-boomin' an' a-blastin at the mob of the day. When that mob's been coaxed into absence even Will Gordon takes flight like the afterthought he is—cryin' an' cursin' himself as his shame starts t'rapidly eclipse his revenge. Wishin' he'd have taken up gun-slingin' 'stead o' pharmacy—half-wishin' he'd had the courage to freeze-dry his grief on the end o' one o' them warnin' volleys whistlin' overhead.

An' when cab's done, he does sort o' a half-twist t'ward them two other stutterin' gats 'at was helpin' him along—an' standin' there proud as a horse's dick at the races is big ned. With galloway jest hidin' 'tween ned's filthy faded originals—awaitin' cab's decree.

cab jest veers in an about-face an' heads back into ma's to wash up, motionin' for trapper dan to wipe the dirt off his facsimile of a face—fixin' him with eyes that so clearly say *pig* that the trapper starts feelin' the end of his nose t'see if it's mor-phosed into a snout from the heat o' cab's glare.

cab's veerin' like that means he's glad that big ned came 'round when he did, maybe glad enough t'even let snake-eyed galloway crawl across the earth for another day. 'Cause cab always shoots them 'at would flee him as soon as he sees 'em—if'n he's gonna shoot at all. He pulls none—'ceptin' his own.

galloway ever-so-thankful to ned. Weren't that a fine idea for ned t'suddenly switch t'wards *helpin'* the otherwise-pre-occupied cabana? (Instead o' pluggin' him from the rear.)

How ever-fuckingly thoughtful of him! How spawn-fucking-taneous. Congratu-fucking-lations!

—We're actually back in his good graces, you an' I, ned—he's grateful! cabana's grateful! Who knows just how useful this new good will towards us may yet turn out to be...

But all big ned's thinkin' about is PUSSY an' his li'l reward—an' he lets his oversized bawd o'erhang the petitionin' galloway as he looms t'be serviced.

But galloway pulls away. In his humble opinion: a clause that might limit the amount payable. The contract specified cabana's life and not some meager act like breaking up an essentially leaderless mob of town simpletons posing as a posse determined to transform a druggist into a sheriff.

But galloway ain't ezackly hankerin' to tell big ned a simple *no dice*—reasonin' that if he does, the far-from-vegetarian ned might just reach down into his throat an' rip his tonsils out an' eat 'em right before him, which'd be a mite distasteful so he simply tells him...

A place. Where to find her. A field 'at galloway really *does* own but which is not the right field—one that's occupied by *faux* cows and Henry Moore sheep that just might lure the ever-tumescent ned away from the cows. Tells ned about this field in con-fie-dential man-to-man whispers, an' wouldn't you know it, the propuhtee is a mere three and a half miles away. Three and a half miles, ned, then *Ouch and O-my!*—she gets to savor your freshly steaming loaf deep inside her.

Ned steams off in search of a far-away girl-on-paper—lumberin' fast as he can albeit dead-opposite to the direction where Louise actually is currently changin' diapers on her whingin' Jamie-boy. An' galloway pens the followin' note in preparation for when ned seethes his way back with even bloodier-shot eyes:

BIG NED: HAROLD GALLOWAY HERE. HAVE GONE TO VISIT TENANT ON ONE OF MY MORE EXTENSIVE HOLDINGS. ANNUAL GENERAL MEETING THIS TIME OF YEAR. WILL RETURN SHORTLY. SORRY I MADE A MISTAKE IN THE DIRECTIONS TO THE GIRL. WHEN I GET BACK, I'LL BE SURE TO GIVE YOU THE RIGHT DIRECTIONS, TO MAKE GOOD AND SURE THAT YOU LOCATE HER. CAN'T YOU JUST TASTE HER?

ON MY WAY TO MY MEETING I'LL DROP IN ON HER. WILL TELL HER TO SPRUCE HERSELF UP REAL NICE DOWN-BELOW FOR YOU.

      EVER YOUR FRIEND AND ASSOCIATE,
      H. GALLOWAY

On his way t'leavin' town—ole sly harold stops in at Carla's bar seein' as it's mornin' and none of the eight are there. Learns from Lucy that Gordon's young son Gary bled to death, real ugly-like—leg caught in a bear trap. Clucks his tongue with an oh-my-Gawd kind o' flavor and composes the followin' note, to druggist Bill Gordon:

DEAR BILL:
HAROLD GALLOWAY HERE. UNSPEAKABLE SORROW ON LEARNING OF YOUR RECENT TRAGIC LOSS. ONE OF MY BUSINESS ASSOCIATES JUST INFORMED ME ABOUT IT. WORDS CANNOT EXPRESS... SUCH THINGS ARE BEYOND CREDULITY, EVEN IN THESE FRAUGHT TIMES. CONDOLENCES TO YOUR FINE WIFE SHEILA. THE DEAR LADY MUST BE BESIDE HERSELF WITH SORROW.

 WILL REDOUBLE OUR EFFORTS AT SAFER NEIGHBORHOODS AND COMMUNITIES. OUR THOUGHTS AND PRAYERS ARE WITH YOU AT THIS TRYING TIME.

      YOURS WITH FOND REGARDS,
      HAROLD GALLOWAY
      ACTING PUBLIC SAFETY MINISTER

But Bill Gordon is dead by the time the note reaches his home, the steel grillwork still tight across the front of his pharmacy weeks later. Never to return to work. Instead, broke through an emergency exit of the biodome, throwin' himself down on the burnin' desert sand and breathin' the ferocious air to his heart's delight—then snuffin' his indignation by blowin' his brains out with a reconditioned revolver he'd been handed by one of the townies before he marched off to ma's.

galloway arranges for Gordon's widow Sheila to stay on for a while in the suite above the store—sort of keep the name Bill Gordon 'round these parts a while longer. Shakes his head over the little bundle of a boy named Gary to whose above-ground-burial funeral he plans to contribute still more o' those new dollars that bear his very own signature.

That's life for you—one endless game of recycling.

katydid, katydidn't

Night.

You can't see dirt at night. Still the added weightiness of cold night air gives the illusion of depth. And fills in another sensation: taste. So that you taste the dark. And it tastes thick.

    henry morgan lying across the sofa, one leg crossed on the other, looking out at the night through the big bulletproof one-way window at ma's, looking over the sprawled bodies of six other sleepers, snoring away in the sound sleep of those who know not what to ask. The window frames the senseless block of black, its stars inconsequential as crumbs—a picture you could look away from easily if there were something else to turn to.

    For a moment his gaze falls on black amos barton, whose ebony skin blends with the room, except for the bluish shine from a line or two in his craggy face. But henry's eyes turn right back towards the night. And are riveted.

    'Til now he hadn't really looked at it. Hours ago he sat there on the polar bear rug binging on thawed Sara Lee cake and savoring the moment. When a voice he knew to be Bill Gordon's croaked out the death-word *cabana*—while henry's gun remained snug in its holster, all that fateful afternoon. How he licked dark chocolate from his fingers without even liking its taste while his ears listened in on what was going down outside. How he'd excused himself and went to the back room to try and nap rather than take a flying leap at the inevitable.

It was tailor-made terror—for an honest druggist who would knock the profit margins off prescriptions whenever someone couldn't come up with the money and who would patiently try to explain to someone with the IQ of a shirt-size exactly how to take their precious medicine. And to think how henry just lay there licking his fingers clean. Finger food. Bugger's banquet.

henry morgan's eyes press shut fighting a soul that wants night-data, that wants to contemplate life outside the high-tech window. His eyes flicker their little night-brushes, their paper-thin walls that have managed to close out so many worst-case scenarios.

But night's fingers ease under eyelids and stretch them open to yank him from the blackout. Tears begin to well up and nearly overrun the barricades. When suddenly he is bailed out—by his ears. Because he can hear the night cry out and its sound takes his mind off everything that took place on the day of the confrontation. What the night says is *Katydid. Katydidn't.* Crickets are using the silence as a backdrop, the silence that traps your sense of awe like a net.

Katydid. Katydidn't. Katydid. Katydidn't.

Right now some trigger-happy crickets are leaping over the white clouds covering the two Gordon corpses, father and son—rubbing their legs together in an old creaky fiddler's number and depriving the bodies of the power that silence bestowed on them. On the roof of an old warehouse other crickets move slowly along the broad wooden beams and beyond. They climb across another bloodied cloth, their bandy legs squealing *Katydid. Katydidn't.* The dried blood on the blanket flakes off as the wind-up crickets pass against it, their every move revealing more and more of the thin, white, blood-marbled meat to the indifferent night. A leg John Gideon stored aloft instead of surrendering it to galloway's self-feeding dry-ice dumpster—a leg there might still be a use for.

Katydid. Katydidn't chirp the crickets of the soul. Columbine to Taber, Virginia Tech to Dawson. Au-ro-ra, dark night Au-ro-ra—Newtown, Newtown, Newtown.

The absurd little to-and-fro soothes henry morgan, so that his eyes finally close and he is whisked away—like some important captured foreign diplomat too powerful to torture—to a land of deep, forgiving sleep.

CORPOREALIZATION

black amos barton and the racial question

Now it might seem kind o' strange to have one black man kickin' up his slinky legs on the coffee table at ma's an' sort of chompin' on a powerful see-gar and laughin' with a lifetime's worth of pearly whites. 'Cause if'n there was only one black man, several questions might come to mind: lak, mebbe he is about t'be e-radicated, seein' as how he is a my-nority group. And if'n that's the case, how does he dare set around chompin' on that ashy volcano o' his, smellin' up ma's drapes an' damn near poisonin' the bread dough with it whenever he struts into the kitchen? His very name *black amos barton* shows that these-here questions of pig-mentation were not en-tirely overlooked.

Still another query pokes up its beady little head: why in the *hill* had black amos b. refrained from bringin' in *other* blacks; I mean why ain't there more than one black in the fust place, given that the community was not entirely closed to their entry? Is he alone on accoun' of tokenism? Or see-lective advertisin'? Does a space-age plastic dome a gated community make?

Well, you take more than a passin' look at black amos barton with an eye to studyin' him an' one thang comes to be purfectly clear: he ain' gonna hang around ma's in any in-fear-ior capacity. He'd only hang out if'n blacks were considered t'be at least a bit *better* 'n whites.

Course cabana's color don't serve as much of a guideline bein' as it's an indeterminate silvery grey varyin' down in spots to rusty russet.

black amos elbowed his way into the big eight six months ago. In them days number eight was a nineteen year old—'bout the age that billy is now and that kid went by the name o' shakey quent. His pre-eight name was Quentin Dirge, but they gave him the name a-fore-mentioned, on accoun'a he was a mite epileptic.

Now, this little malady was put up with for quite a while. Any group 'at can hack the likes of trapper dan won't fret too much over a bit o' harmless cryin' out, fallin' down an' shiverin' an' shakin' an' such, 'specially when quent would usually fore-warn everyone present with a bit of an aura, consistin' of *awe shee-yit! Here it comes—duck!*

So quent's membership went on in good-enough standin' 'til one day the eight were 'bout t'set down to table with ma, when quent wen' on one of his little tremor-binges straight-off *without* no aura and in the process knocked over a bowl of pipin' hot to-mato soup onto cabana's munificent lap.

cab didn't say much—he sort o' smiled as the steam ate its way into his legs an' rose in a billow from his now see-through buckskins. Didn't say much at all. But the next day in Carla's bar on the bullshittin' board there was this announcement:

VACANCY BEIN' CONSIDERED IN BIG EIGHT.
ONLY FAST GUNS NEED APPLY (NO MUTATIONS, PLEASE).
FOR MORE—*HIT QUENT*.
harold galloway
EXECUTIVE ADMINISTRATOR to the big eight

Two days later—bet yo' ass no one else had the moxie to apply—Black Amos Barton (still bearin' the stigma o' capitals) rode up to ma's decked out in a eight-hundred-dollar royal-blue silk blousey shirt with a vest half-cotton, half-ramie and spurs of pure silver astride his appropriately Manichean white mare. The horse—formerly an Appaloosa—had had the gray painted over with Wite-Out, and Barton held the pommel of his saddle and leaned wayyy back—crackin' the odd joke or two as if he were high-sidin' and low-ridin' through a Cleveland slum in a repossessed Cadillac Escalade.

He waited outside ma's nearly an hour or two—roastin' a bit o' beans an' reclinin' on a field of indoor-outdoor—an' knew eggzackly what he was waitin' *fer*, havin' heard from ole galloway that whenever quent went into one of his fits, the nearest of the big seven would grab him by the seat o' his pants an' throw him outside for to let the malady run its course—far away from the food. At about twelve noon—about five minutes after henry morgan switched on ma's fluorescent strobe bug-light and told quent to watch it fer him fer a while—quent begun to fly off the handle, an' bloody willy jumped up an' slid a knife into his mouth between his teeth though galloway's doctor-book recommended a pencil, an' willy an' ned sort o' escorted quent to the door then heaved him outside for a round o' twitchin' an' firin' like a long roll of ladyfingers.

Outside while quent was a-shakin' and a' squirmin' an' flippin' over like a flapjack in heat, Black Amos B. dis-mounted from his tall horse, kind of sidled up to shakey quent and drawled smoothly: —Draw.

Well quent's hands may have started t'shake towards his guns as barton claims they did, an' mebbe he did make a bold try t'sort of balance one of his guns a bit 'cept within a second he had four or five bullet holes in him an' was more or less pre-occupied with shakin' while his blood ran in rivulets into the gully—as though he was some sheep's-gut bag o' wine some drunken cowpoke or psyched-up cop had jest peppered with lead. Then amos b. kind of blew into the barrels of his pearl-studded guns, wiped 'em clean an' walked real slow into ma's winkin'—inquirin' o' the other seven who the lawn-sprinkler outside belonged to.

Now from the start things was a bit strained on accoun' a the only black that ma's place had even seen was this smilin' old jokester named Tom who came to dee-liver the "milk" once a week—one of them galloway food substitutes that tasted like a combeenation of liquid plastic, Chinese melamine and water'd-down soy. Well whatever imp-ression that fella with the winkin' ivories might've given o' black men was somewhat suddenly erased when amos shot him thirteen times—sort of hastenin' his re-tirement for the sake of eliminatin' stereo-types and pushin' reset on future race relations.

'Til now the question of color had never even bothered to come up, seein' as how two things were true of the eight: First, no one could tell what the *hell* color dan was 'cause the trapper was always covered in mud of some kind or t'other. Second henry morgan, the older eight cousin, plum-near as old as galloway some said—who had busted his way into the eight jest a short time earlier—turned out to be a mite unusual anatomically, like he could also be a member of some my-nority group. 'Cause it was ob-served in the shower room that he was missin' the li'l curtain off his centerpiece. Why once fat-ass jake en-quired —Jest why's yores shaped so different from evuhbaddy else's? To which henry smiled sort of defensive-like an' answered —Cut myself shavin'.

Moreovuh only henry referred to *it* swingin' back and forth by the unwesternly term of *salami,* which he later X-plained to the other seven was the name of an Oriental belly dancer he scored with in Bag-dad.

So the rumor that mebbe henry was a mumbo-jumbo Huguenot or a Romney Mormon or even worse a Jyoo—these various types of creatures emanatin' from the my-norities index of one of galloway's debriefin' papers—set up for the eight a kind of what's-the-point approach to individual differences so that they settled for acceptin' jest about anythin' that proved hardy enough to survive around ma's.

Even touchy things like sexual myths or other such stories about blacks weren't strong enough t'cause heads t'turn at ma's. Shee-yit ain't no black gonna bring down a neighborhood with the likes of trapper dan or big ned sloughin' around. Moreovuh the myth that blacks spent everythin' on their horses and outfits and near-nothin' on their homes didn't trouble no one here since everyone 'cept ned and henry morgan and o' course cab lived at ma's place anyhoo. Last o' all: the myth that niggers have the biggest kaboos was jest blown to crap whenevuh cabana swung by. Though perhaps tellin'ly, only barton kept on his bulgin' boxershorts—even in the shower—sort of keepin' down the provocation of the man he knew was boss and we ain't talkin' hugo neither.

town hall meetin'

It's on again—again for the sixth time someone worked up the nerve to get the townsfolk together to decide "once and for all" just what to do about the shoot-ups and the intimidation, the drunkenness and the late-night panda-monium. But this time it's different. This time there's town blood on the agenda. The blood of a young boy.

As usual the meetin' is held in the huge wheat arena, an enormous drafty field of a buildin' connected to the dome by a single-layer plastic tunnel—where everyone has to wear a warm coat, and indignation seeps out in steamy breath, condensin' in the frigid air of the desert night. Again as usual the chairman is none other than harold galloway, MBA. LLD. Or, so he claims, the only man remotely fa-miliah with "pah-lamentary proceedyuh" who can talk about as pah-tickulahly as a Canadian weenie educated in the You-Ess-of-A at Hah-vahd Yahd or someone who jest come back from a stint at Ox-ford as a Rhodesy.

—Ahem. Let us now call the roll—galloway's high-falootin' way o' sayin, *Let's jest have us a roll call.* And the group of townsfolk at the head table—a couple of fold-out bridge tables set end-to-end topped by a long sheet o' plywood covered over with a tablecloth—each nod as their names are called. At the foot of the oversize wooden stage, the audience of men matched by their respective women is shiverin' but keen enough to call out or at least mumble *Here!* when their surnames ring out in the crisp night air.

Meetin's keep everybody up late—even as late as the big ones stay out gamblin', and no one will make any noise when they file out the arena doors afterwards for fear of drawin' the big ones away from Carla's fo' some target practice. Everyone always comes away feelin' real darin' and rebellious fo' even havin' *bin* at such a meetin': some of them are armed with only the keys to their quaint wooden prefabs—aluminum sidin' really—where their children are hidden away dreamin' o' shoot-outs on creaky-springed mattresses, incorporatin' day residue as dreamers are wont to do.

About half the fold-down chairs around the center aisle headin' towards the stage are occupied by mutations in their Stryker-frames and wheelchairs—some o' 'em makeshift affairs, some with fake plasma drips. None of 'em able to string together more than a half-dozen words.

—Mr. Shulberg...

—Here, mister "chairman," said sarcastic-like. —And oh yes, lest I forget, age forty-five.

—Mr. Dodson...

—Right, age forty-five.

—Mr. Kelly and Mr. Mounds...

Kelly and Mounds in chorus: —Here. Forty-five and forty-five.

—Mrs. Birch, Mrs. Kelly, Mrs. Taylor, Mrs. Mounds...

Mrs. Taylor for the lot of them: —Here, mr. chairman; all ages forty-five, give er take...

And so on until: —Mrs. William Gordon, wife of the late William Gordon.

A lull then a murmur as a widow stands up blackly.

Sheila Gordon: —Here in body alone. Age fifty-five.

—I beg your pardon, Mrs. G., but you must have that incorrect. galloway tries to remember if he'd forgotten to come by and check her innoculation' log...

—Alright then, have it your way, forty-five. But I'm feelin' one hell of a lot older than the rest of these mid-lifers...

Which kind of queers galloway's usual opener about how nice it is that the audience all have one thing in common—bein' of the same generation o' baby boomers—and how when *he* was that age... By-the-by he recalls that he *did* stop to check on Mrs. G.'s treatment—her pre-treatment personality must be breakin' through. Only shows the limits of medical farm-ocology...

galloway hits the agenda runnin'. The first item is the Gordon double-funeral. He publicly offers to pay a substantial portion of the cost. Murmurs of *How kind!* from some, *Stands to reason!* from a few pair of well-chewed lips.

Next item is the methods to be used to prevent such tragic mishaps from occurin' in the future, and the floor is open to suggestions.

No one says shit. No sense originatin' ideas only to have 'em vetoed. All eyes riveted on galloway. A huge communal silence builds in the echo chamber.

—Very well, then. If there are no constructive suggestions, then I, uh, shall make a proposal. Ladies and gentleman—gettin' it up now, he is—we should undertake Emergency Measures from this day on to scrutinize the residential *as well as* the downtown areas for bear traps and related hazards. Well-regulated minutiae being necessary to the security of our free state, I move that an assistant to Mr. Parkinson, who has to this day performed his duties so ably in the downtown area, be appointed to a second zone, and be put on town salary at once.

Then silence as a big curly haired carpenter-type name o' Gideon rises high on his shanks, walks t'wards the front and bellows in a boomin' dare-all: —Ain't that a trifle *moderate, mister* galloway?

Folks are wary of Gideon: self-named Bible thumper—still there's mumblin', buzzin' and whisperin'. With galloway doin' a *Robert's Rules of Order*: —If I may answer Mr. Gideon's question.

—Accusation, says Gideon.

—Whatever, be so good as to permit me to explain my reasoning.

—Would that your hand were on a Bible as you did.

galloway pays no more heed to this than to a belch. Bible types will be Bible types. —Now I've heard a lot of foolhardy talk floating around here lately about trying to run the big eight out of town or sending for some outside help, though from *where* that might *possibly* come is beyond the scope of this meeting. Think globally but *act locally* and all that. What I *can* say is: *that* kind of talk, that only leads to more deaths—more and more Bill Gordons.

—My son wasn't killed because of town resistance, mr. galloway...

—Now, please, Mrs. Gordon. We all know what you must be going through, and we—

—He was *killed* because some godless hooligan laid an insane and purposeless trap... There are no bears here...never have been! And she breaks down with galloway hammerin' his gavel to prevent the other townsmen from takin' up the bit.

—Miss-us Gordon, bear traps in themselves do not kill people. Accidents and improper storage of bear traps are what kill people. Why blame the poor, inanimate bear trap?

—Where have I heard that before?

—Before I continue, let me apologize on behalf of our recently bereaved, for her understandably forceful language—now *please*! Let me finish what I have to say, then you can come to a decision *as a town*...

—Ain't you *part* of the town too, galloway, or are you somewheres else?

—Or *somethin'* else!

Cries of *Sneak! Imposter! Accomplice!* go 'round as galloway fakes losin' it —I SHALL HAVE TO ADJOURN THIS MEETING AS ITS CHAIRMAN, UNLESS WE HAVE ORDER IMMEDIATELY! galloway's version of *Clam up, ciphers*. Never uses five words when ten'll do. —AND PLEASE, MR. GIDEON, TAKE YOUR SEAT OR WE SHALL NEVER REMAIN ON SCHEDULE.

—Thank you. Now, my point is that getting the big eight out of ma's—or wherever else they decide to take over—will cost this town a substantial number of lives, whether it's sheriffs' or townspeople's lives...

—Aren't sheriffs *paid* to take that kind of risk? jeers Kelly.

—*Unless*, IF YOU'LL ALLOW ME TO CONTINUE, MR. KELLY, *UNLESS* we try to deal with the most mature, the most thoughtful of the big eight, a man who will hear us out *AND* who just might be able to talk the big eight out of their ways...

—Who might that man be, other than Jesus Christ? challenges Gideon, his remark followed by a wave of nervous laughter. None of 'em are used to laughin' along with Gideon, who is always above needin' support.

—Or maybe big ned? comes from some five-and-dimer in the back row.

Humor, last refuge of the helpless. Second only to astrology and lottery tickets. —As a matter of fact, this voice of reason in the eight is on his way right this minute to talk with us—

People's heads turn towards the huge arena doorway, cranin' to look for the mystery guest who terrifies by dint o' bein' a member of the eight.

Sheila Gordon calls out —Fool! What if when he comes in, he brings his *friends* with him! This is the chance they've been waitin' for—kill us all at once! To which there's a whole lot of nervous shufflin'.

—Now don't go gettin' hysterical, my dear—not a single one of the eight wants to harm anyone in this room, and that includes *you know who*. They have a pretty sick sense of fun—I'll grant you that—but the only people they ever up an' *murder* is *each other*. Why, if they ever did come after a town's person, it'd be yours truly, since I'm the one taking up town causes...

Some spittin' in the back rows. —Cut the crap, galloway and tell us who this special phil-anthrope of yours is, who can have a heart an' still manage to ride with the eight. Somehow none of us can think of one...

—henry morgan.

—*henry morgan!* That *turncoat*! That overgrown yuppy with the silver hair—who was once a distinguished member of the human race—who left a lovely wife and a thriving medical practice to join these terrible-twos for little more than sex and cheap thrills! cries Mrs. Gordon herself from the front-row seat she's moved up to. —He would know about indecency, all right. It's his *new way of life*...

—Now, that's just your *opinion*, Mrs. Gordon, says galloway, lookin' to the rear door an' moppin' his brow with a hanky.

—Well, who else is talking, Joan of Arc? Point is: henry morgan is into scaring all his old friends, yet he's the only one of the whole bunch of them that's old enough to *know* better—why, some say he's pushing *your* age.

—Checkmate, then, my good townspeople. So mister morgan's a hound. Would you rather we all try an' appeal to *cabana*? Maybe benefit from the bounty of his *under twenty years* of wisdom?

Silence. Stone-faced dread across their faces. cabana: the phrase that pays...*Boko Haram...Islamic State...The ISIS crisis...*

—Sometimes I think if cabana didn't exist, you would've invented him.

—That will be enough of that, dear! Rest assured, good townsfolk, that one day we'll have enough officers out there on the streets to be able to put behind bars *anyone under twenty* who handles a gun in an irresponsible manner.

—Why not just confiscate the guns...*and* the ammo...*and* while you're at it...the bear traps? challenges Sheila Gordon. —You have the means...

—Nai-eve remarks like that don't merit a response. We don't have time tonight to review our long frontier past, or the meaning to a man of his personal piece.

—The right to arm bears, heckles some five-and-dimer. —It's a misreadin' of the Constitution! The second *half* of the Second Amendment!

—Well, then, it was one heck of a mis-reading, says galloway, because it's inscribed high on a wall at what's left of NRA headquarters in Fairfax, Virginia. It helped put 300 million guns in civilian hands. The degree of gun control I've achieved for us is a *damned* sight better than that. But there, now you've got *me* using cuss words.

Just as a sullen silence floats through the arena—thick as a beer fart no one's willin' to take credit for—galloway sets to pour himself a glass of water an' spills half of it as the huge oak doors suddenly swing open.

An' there between aisles of nervous people shufflin' their feet and mutations droolin' even more than usual is henry morgan—coolly stridin' in with not a trace of a stoop in his still-muscular back, hands far off his guns and an expression o' determination on his face like he is thinkin' about somethin' far-off and important-like: If you look deep enough in concentration, no one'll try to plug you or even pick a fight with you. Most guys will break a face sooner than dare to break a man's train of thought.

As henry takes the stage, the town baker—who just watched the crease on the back of henry's pants as he strode by—whispers into the ear of the town plumber sittin' next to him: —If we get him in the back now, there'll be only seven to deal with.

—N-naw, stutters the plumber who in a past life was a receivables clerk in a shippin' room. —Let's s-s-save it for on his way out, when he's right up close—t-t-two bullets each.

morgan unwinds his bandana, wipes the galloway-germs off the Scandinavian cut-glass, takes a long swig o' water—half-sensin' how much his belly'd be leakin' if he turned away fer long—and waves off the chairman who was fixin' to introduce him.

—Listen good. I ain't here to intimidate. I didn't bring these guns for that purpose, but I figured I might need 'em 'cause I know I'm none too popular around here. An' the first thing I want t'address is the reason *why*.

—My husband and boy murdered and you're not *popular!* from Mrs. Gordon, who's calmed down by Schulberg the banker—a mellow forty-five.

—I aim to get to that Sheila—though let's keep things straight: your husband was not *murdered*, though yer son did die an awful death.

Murmurs: —How *dare* he...

—Y'see the reason my stock isn't too high here—contrary to wide opinion—is not because I up an' joined the eight. The reason is that at my age I should know better than t'be traipsin' aroun' with those hulkin' specimens; I even heard your kid back there—points to the plumber Barker, who plans to plug him after the speech—your own kid sayin' that nobody likes morgan because he isn't half the gunman that cabana or big ned is—he's a "poser," nothin' more than a promoted town man who's kept his looks. Same goes for black amos barton. Now where d'ya think he picked up ideas like *those*? Mebbe you should start makin' up yer minds—

do ya hate me for *bein'* a gunman or 'cause I'm *not enuff* o' one...

—If you look at yourselves real-hard you'll find you have a secret *admiration* for the eight, and mebbe it's that admiration that's standin' in yore way—mebbe *that's* what gives the eight their power over you.

Righteous rumblin's permeate the room as morgan goes on.

—Mebbe it's yore secret love of gun-totin' warriors 'at brought this whole world to ruin in the first place, 'at makes you despise li'l ole chicken-hawk here. Points to galloway who's sweatin' from his hair to the tassels on his dress shoes and who sticks a small white fast-acting Xanax under his tongue for extra pluck. —You made him yore chairman because you admire his pee-kyoo-liar ability to survive around the eight.

galloway ghostly white, sits his bony ass down on a bridge-chair, relieved that morgan didn't say that *he made himself* your chairman', which would blow the democracy ruse. A fine point, and yet...

—*Cut the parlor-Freud pep talk, morgan...*

—Now, I ain't tellin' you this so's you'll understand yoreselves— 'cause quite frankly it was my boredom with you-all that drove me to join the eight in the first place—er, the fust place. But if you think about it you'll decide yore as responsible for the murders aroun' here as the eight are.

—My, my, my...*mister* glib-and-slick morgan, how *con*-venient, calls out Sheila Gordon, who's turnin' into a mighty effective heckler in her widowhood. —When in doubt, share the blame—is that it?

—Share the *responsibility* is more like it. Don't gimme yore helpless victims *shtick*—

—What are you suggesting *mister*, not Doctor Morgan*stern?* challenges John Gideon. —That we all look into our deepest, darkest selves, as a way of more effectively *going after* the eight—that we *forgive* them as a bunch of godforsaken numbskulls, even forgive the one man among them who *ought to know better*, but who just needed a bit o' relief from a real *bad* case of boredom... You're just as godless as Hollywood ever was... I happen to have with me this worn Bible, and just the right passage from Corinthians...

—Spare us your Gospel of bygone days... It did nothin' to keep us from gettin' to the mess we're in today. It didn't stop the milit'rization of earth *or* the heavens! I respect a man of yore obvious physical abilities for *not* joinin' the eight—though there haven't 'xactly been any openin's lately...

henry pauses. —I'm *not* advocatin' that you take up arms against the eight, 'cause I know you'd all be deader 'n door-stops if you did. But I think you've got some homework t'do, so you can git some kind of collective power equal to what the eight now have. I mean, you got to get rid of the things that keep you little people...lookin' at gideon... *Here's* one who's well over six feet tall, yet lugs a Bible with 'im everywhere he goes—like a security blankie.

—What do you carry *with you*? chimes the pit-bull diva Sheila Gordon. —Your precious piece? Your re-issued "man card"?

—Is that why Gary Gordon was killed? Because he was a little person? coughs up ole Doc Halverson, another one who looks real old but has managed t'keep his marbles.

—The death of Gary Gordon was a tragic thing—it kept me up for nights on end wishin' I was dead myself an' feelin' about as guilty as a man might feel...

—Without *doin'* beans about it... How *could* you just *sit* there inside ma's while...

—Because Sheila Gordon, ain't no great good gonna come from me gettin' blown t'bits by cabana. It wouldn't put back your son's leg and it wouldn't have made his pappy Will Gordon any more sensible...

More righteous indignation: How *dare* he...

—henry, our own Doctor Morganstern, how in God's name can you remain a member of those...

—Because Sheila, bein' one of you and bein' powerless is not an option. The old world order is over. Even if they used to call it the *New World Order* an' our ole prezeedent was smack-dab in the middle of it— hey! Now, you jest set back now Hal, 'cause I see what you're up to—ask y'selves not what gives me the right to be big, but why you all are so determined to stay small. Why not corral papa galloway here and ask him how he manages to get from the eight *whatever the hell he wants*—get him to twist around his methods 'til they're straighter forward, then you'll see how powerful a whole town can be, even if half its citizens *are* sick an' gettin' sicker.

—Yeah, and who's gonna keep us in breathable air an' drinkable water way galloway's been doin'—you? You got the *science* for that? Derisive laughter.

—Yeah, says morgan, noddin', I guess crusty old harold has us all by the science. Excuse me if I can't see my way clear t'bein' one of his distinguished medical staff, he takes a dig, pickin' out Doc Halverson who looks down at his shoes.

—mister morgan, I have not invited you here today to *add fuel to the fire*...

But morgan's guns spin at the *mister*—a mock Colt .45 in each hand with the action of a Glock or Beretta—and he holds 'em straight in front of galloway's pill-speckled face.

—You clam the fuck *up*, Mr. Airsoft. I'm not gonna make the same mistake cabana's making—of treatin' you as unfair game just because you're unarmed and wear a tie; I know you hemorrhoidal corporate types galloway—I know bein' cruel comes natural to you...

The baker an' plumber both bolt up real-quick, haulin' sawed-off shot guns out from under their coats as morgan spins like a carnival wheel, firin' bullets that graze their calloused hands, drawin' screams as their weapons fly out of those hands like soft machines—lost promises...

morgan backs down the steps, off the stage and down the aisle—guns up front, straight out the doorway, addin' insult as he goes:
—You're all blowin' it...*again*...drivin' away yore only honest link with the eight in yourselves—

—You save it! cry the peanuts, an' Doc Halverson rushes open his bag to help the wounded. galloway scribbles a memo and soon he's supervisin' the evacuation of the wounded and their wives, who are oh *honey*in' them, an' then poundin' his gavel for some order.

From John Gideon: —May the Lord Jesus Christ forgive that unrepentant sinner, to which he supplies his own *Amen*. —He has the nerve to claim he hails from an Abrahamic faith! Wander on, thou faithless heathen.

When the crowd settles, great Gideon rises up and moves that the town send old galloway himself as a personal messenger to the eight, with some concrete proposals—but galloway rules him out of order on a pro-ceed-yural mattuh an' the entire town, even the mutations, c'n only sit back an' laugh. An' laugh.

Even Sheila Gordon is a-laughin' 'til she's cryin', and it's welcome that laugh 'cause it loosens the tension and some of the men's wives found the meetin' mighty depressin' 'til now.

Morris Schulberg the banker manages a motion that galloway does let through: —I move that the town bring in cavalry, and I myself am willing to foot half the bill—or perhaps the town can haul in the country's acting head of Homeland See-curity to the next town-hall meetin', jest fly him in t'hear his advice-like…

The town vote on that unlikely motion—'cause the hour is so late—is you-nanimous. 'Cept for two li'l abstentions, namely Gideon and Mrs. Sheila Gordon, red-eyed but without tears now—dry-eyed an' dry-brained enough t'know there ain't no cavalry out there. No see-curity either.

An' the town feels its problem's on the way t'bein' solved, what with a *bona fide* help as good as on his way—and on Schulberg's money yet—and cavalry armed with huge raffles an' bullits an' handsome turned-up mustaches ridin' hard like in a Kevin Costner epic gone *way, way* over budget… Everyone jest wants to git on home 'cause the big ones'll soon be out—when galloway opines that they're not through yit 'cause there's still one small issue left t'deal with.

—There's an item of business that an indecent man might just run by himself and not bother t'consult the townfolk 'bout. But I aim to maintain full respect for this here body.

—Hurry up, galloway, our kids are locked in at home—alone. And people here are hurtin'…

—There's a young girl with neither father nor mother campin' on my lands—she's been hidin' away with a small baby she can't possibly care for...and...

—What's the matter, galloway—you worried you can't co-llect taxes from her, ha ha—

—Or from the baby, ha ha ha.

—Order, order. Let's not be cynical! I ask this town council to approve my calling in a reputable adoption agency to safely remove the little one before both the girl and the baby come to harm.

—Wait! A strong call from a faint voice.

—What now, Sheila?

—I'll take her in—gladly; you just arrange to have her brought to me. My house is feelin' mighty empty...

—But Sheila, you can't be up for...

—I'll decide what I'm up for! I said I'll take her; what more do you need?

And a vision floats by in galloway's mind—of big ned returnin' from his goose chase in the mood to cook some goose...

But it's late an' the town is shufflin', and any chairman knows what t'do once murmurs can't be gaveled away.

—Thank you, Mrs. Gordon, on behalf of the town, and *wait!* Everybody sit down and let me properly adjourn this meeting. But they remain standin' and some take to movin' for the arena doors—passin' by the little refreshments stand next to where the wounded were tended to just a moment ago. Steppin' past warm droplets of fresh blood soakin' into the wood floor. The whispers die down the moment they enter the damp tunnel system t'start walkin' like race-walkers for to git home afore the silhouettes of big ones gallop by headin' for ma's or wherever else they go for the few hours of sleep they need to recharge 'em.

galloway alone now in the huge eerie space, cursin' himself for his misguided decision to invite morgan. *Might as well invite John Gideon to preach.* Pours another glass o' water an' sits down on the center stage and remembers that most of the town is due for their injections next week. But all he can think about is ned's forearms—that look more like thighs. ned who can barely read the thoughtfully worded note he left him. (ma will help him out Montessori-like.) ned who's likely fixin' "t'torture him fust"—a'fore killin' him cruelly with the hairy fielder's mitts 'at only his own mamaw would call hands. An' galloway just sippin' at his water, starin' out the doorway for the light to come in an' eventually say *Mohnin'*—lettin' him know that still more time has run out.

At least mine are temporary setbacks; at least I know who I am—not like that refugee from mid-life mr. henry m., the erstwhile good Doctor Henry Morganstern. Here I sit, a billionaire, craving the likes of that imposter as a friend. How pathetic I must have looked standing next to morgan (since when do they grow Jews that big?)—with that goddamn bulge in those pretentiously laced buckskins. galloway looks down at his tweed dress slacks—*slacks* is the right word—flatter than a pancake at the crotch, an' reaches down into his pocket t'gather up a couple hazelnuts and push 'em forward in imitation. Then stares at the tassels on his Guccis only to shake his head, grit his teeth and remember: that's just how the world fell apart in the first place. It was the inability of other men to back down from the brink of destruction that gave him, harold the great galloway, the run of this little horror-show.

I invited morgan to be part of my technosphere, but he chose to be part of the entertainment underneath these leaky domes. It was a mid-life thing. To be durable enough to survive—an underrated virtue.

An' he pours himself a splash of coffee from the urn at the end of the stage—an urn so empty you'd think it was the tail-end of an AA meetin'— sippin' it with a teaspoon (why risk a burned lip?) and then in a move straight out of a spaghetti Western, he spins around like henry m., his hands reachin' for imaginary guns. Then chucks his stainless spoon clear-down on the wood floor where it skips a few times and hits a front-row seat. Then freezes with a *shee-yit!* an' vows t'try on a pair of his very own buckskins real soon in a securely latched fittin' room in one of his underground-mall stores—the kind 'at has a mirror inside each fittin' room so you don't have to give a little fashion show in front of the sales clerks, let alone the other customers.

Once I was king of FaceTime and Instagram, lord of the conference call, maven of all apps, master of one. Showing up in person was for losers: I had outreach!

Reaches for the outside pocket of his murse, jest to remember there ain't no cell phone there, an' words lak *wireless* are no longer the purview of everyman.

All the while knowin' he's gettin' carried away—carryin' on, like an unsung, unrecognized member of the eight. *The price you pay for mixing with the entertainment...*

carla's purr

As henry morgan ambles back t'ward Carla's, he gives little thought to how his havin' been away must've looked—his havin' taken leave of a card game he'd been *winnin'* with a simple *Scuse me boys* and struttin' off into the night to visit his wife or do somethin' equally wussy.

He isn't thinkin' about much else other than how nasty it was to have had to inflict flesh wounds on two townsmen to whom he would've once givin' tetanus shots.

He passes by some dozy-lookin' housies you could enter through exits in the tunnel system and a few storefronts boarded up for the night and the bank and the general store—nothin' specific sold there—each piece o' property straight off a Monopoly board, each geared more towards some Disney concept of the Wild Wild West or the cover of a Zane Grey novel. 'Til he comes to a steel door marked *Authorized Personnel Only*. Once through, it's only a ten minute walk to the outskirts and Carla's saloon with them deep-brown, heavy-swingin' oak doors—doors that keep swingin' for an hour after you walk through 'em.

He flings them open nice 'n definitively and comes upon the big ones—all 'cept for big ned—sittin' there in a circle—jest flickin' kings, queens 'n aces, sippin' whiskey an' peerin' out the brims o' their hats for Cahhh-la.

Soon's henry comes in, Carla eases herself off the tabletop, flows towards the beer tap 'n pours him some foamy like cabana himself had directed her to do so. But henry just stands at the end of the crowded table without quite re-assumin' his place—his hands at his guns in a pre-conversant stance as he surveys the game play and awaits his cue.

Then spots a huge vanadium hand arcin' a dirk of a first finger.

C'mere is the motion and the finger is cabana's...

The rest of 'em appear ab-sorbed in playin'. fat-ass jake (no bluffer) yellin' *Feck it!* as he sizes up his hand, but the others for the most part posin', half-watchin' t'see how henry reacts to his callin' as he moseys on closer to card land. henry coolly re-claims his seat on cabana's right in a chair which has grown icy cold of late—though no one's yet struck up a search committee t'fill it. And just says —Deal me in.

Silence and lack o' motion at Carla's. The bar-kitten herself frozen-still at the beer tap, her slender hand cupped around a shot-glass, waitin' for news to break. Lucy is out back in the kitchen thawin' frozen potatoes, and when she walks in jest about to call out Carla's name, she is struck by the silent frame as cab's eyes pierce straight ahead an' she drops her potatoes, fallin' down in a faint, her head crashin' onto the keys of the player piano.

cab freezes the automaton keys into one of them deserted desert silences—the kind that ned might break with a beer fart to the giniral mirth of everyone who'd all simultaneously reach for their noses and guffaw sayin' *OK, who died?* Anyone junior to ned who'd try that would end up with a few extra blowholes out the backside for his trouble.

henry places one of his hands like ginger on the table while the other slides snail-slowly around his belt. Feelin' sweat startin' to lake around the temples jest inside the hat brim.

An' cab's eyes swerve t'wards henry, on henry, as he gives his sandpaper chin a trapezoidal stroke an' opens his thin bloodless lips just a smidge so that slidin' out through gaps in his shark teeth comes *a look* as if t'say:

Where ya bin?

henry feelin' kind of dizzy—as if there was old wax leanin' on his eardrums in need of an Ear-Nose-and-Throat man with a stainless steel curette—tries to look up at the gleam radiatin' from cabana's direction, halfway succeedin' as he lifts his second hand—now heavy as lead—off his buckle an' onto the table with his first. Jest sort o' puts 'em both t'gether an' leans his silvery *GQ* mane forward, restin' his chin on folded hands of confident non-belligerance. Takes a deep slow hatha-yoga breath an' says in a steady voice: —cab Ah been at the town-hall meetin'.

An' cab don't say nothin'. Jest sort of smiles, gives a nod t'wards the wall-eyed Lucy whose head stirs in Carla's lap—she reads the *All Clear* and eases back up on wobbly legs to allow Carla t'fetch henry his beer while black amos barton deals him back in.

Soon it's right-noisy again with jake doin' *hee-haws*, billy goofin' like a kid with every card he gits, and black amos flashin' his priceless set of ivories whenever he wins a hand.

cab jest sippin' at a googol of whiskey, refrainin' from usin' those God-awful eyes 'at can win him a hand whenever he wants 'em to. Carla has Lucy up and around, creepin' through the back room sippin' coffee. With bloody willy burpin' up his drink at trapper dan who's been laughin' an' sloshin' 'round near an hour's worth of burpin's himself. As willy hollers —Kam 'n set with us 'n give us a bit of thet lucky purr o' yores, Missy Cahhhlaa—

Carla smiles an' reproachfully gives her lush 'n loose mane a bit of a shake 'n walks the minefield of men for another night. Headin' straight-on towards each one, she can sense the heat of their glarin'. And when she comes to refill their glasses, she does it slow an' deliberate. As she leans to fill cabana's drink high, she e-mits that little purrrr. Her smile facin' up t'wards one of cabana's three profiles. But with her eyes on henry morgan.

honesty

henry morgan pounds at the door of his wife's place, his own place. At 4:30 a.m., the card game over and the other seven long gone to ma's. Then Claire's hoarse whisper: —henry morgan, enough with the "shave-and-a-haircut" knock. Find a better time to visit!

—Goddamn it, Claire, don't be coy. Lemme in.

—Coy! Did it ever dawn on you, "morgan," that maybe I've had it with you. That it's more a decision of the gut than the heart to never want to see you again! My eyes are achin', so for God's sake—leave. A pause. —Or promise if I let you in, you'll go straight to bed and not bother me.

—Ah, the wiles of long marriage, when fondlin' her derriere becomes buggin' her ass...

—You'll be a lot funnier in six hours, she says, and starts to lock the window shutters.

—Go on, abuse me... Why don't you give me some really far-fetched excuse like you can't see me 'cause you don't want to wake *the kids*...

—What did you say?! And she opens the shutters to glare at him, her head venturing out the window. —What did you say? Monster!

—Okay, okay that was the whiskey talkin'. Let's not do Sid 'n Nancy here.

—henry, you keep taunting me about our infertility... Why?

—I don't know why I always aim low. Just let me in, so I don't have to *break in...*

—For Chrissake, wait 'til I slip on a robe.

morgan holds his tongue.

And she opens wide. 'n he walks in cool, undoin' his holster carelessly and flingin' it over the back of the sofa.

—Dammit! Don't throw those weapons around like that! You know I can't stand it!

morgan mutters to himself.

—Sorry isn't good enough...

Goddamn junkie-nerves. Her eyes are always bloodshot these days—beautiful as they still are—and she's carryin' less weight than she looks good at. She can't be gettin' much exercise in here all day.

She heads for the kitchen to brew him some coffee as he tries again.

—You know, Claire—Claire, can you hear me in there? It felt good a moment ago t'hear you talkin' about slippin' into a bathrobe. And it feels real nice t'have you frettin' about makin' coffee and the like. I guess, well...

—You guess that maybe there's *something* that you miss while you're down there at That Woman's.

—Now, don't go finishin' mah sentences.

—I'm really honored that there's still *some* joy in seeing your own wife...that you're not totally happy every waking hour you spend away from me.

—You through?

—Maybe I should've said *those women*—after all, there's ma, ma who can out-cook me, out-bake me, an' who knows jest WHAT other things she can do better 'n me, henry—or are those feminine functions the sole preserve of your li'l Mizzy Cahhhluh...?

—You *through?*

—Yes.

—Then wipe yourself. Now, pour my coffee and hear me out...

—Can I say something too? she asks.

—What do you mean?

—I mean, after missing you for days on end, can I get out a word of *my* admittedly less important feelings before you start speaking *your* piece?

—Yeah, sure, o' course. I expect you to feel it when I'm away on these long—and I know they have been long—

—Desertions.

—I was going to say *gigs* but *desertions* will do. No more than long games o' golf would be, though, I reckon.

—Golf? Why not? Good t'hear you admit it, henry, about the deserter part and all. Hands him a mug of re-warmed coffee. Talk. And talk more the way you *used to*, please.

morgan back on his feet. —I don't see it Claire. This coldness. Why? You know as well as I do. The way things turned out, we should be happy just to be here...

—henry, henry, poor henry-boy, you're upset with me being "cold." Translation: I'm not going to get all wild-eyed just because you deign to pay me, your own wife, a visit...

Deign? Where she get a word like that? She's been readin' and it's startin' to rub off...

— You come in here in the middle of the night all trussed up in rawhide, like a Wall Street broker at a costume party, and wonder why it doesn't take my breath away...(Checkin' the kitchen quartz, she fakes a yawn. Is she fakin'?) —Just because you could make some dumb blue-eyed strawberry blonde turn red with desire... A fellow mid-lifer like me needs more than a ten-minute romp on the kitchen floor, with or without an ice-cube prep.

He smiles: a Wall Street broker at a costume party? Nice. Is this the woman I regret bein' married to?

—Besides, you know those shots galloway gives me knock me out for hours longer than I used to sleep, and quite frankly (yawns again)—*shee-yit, she is tired*—I've just about had it for tonight, even if you did come here expecting to soothe your guilt with a little speech, followed by some quick, affectionate pity sex. Reties the belt on her robe.

—Cut the jaded-missus crap, Claire. If you're tryin' to hurt me you're succeedin'.

—Poor *bayyy-by*! Will you never stop piling on your endless epic, the tragedy of Henry Morganstern—who had it all, but somehow that wasn't quite enough, whose pain is so much more intense than everyone else's. Your little *I'm sorrys* are as useful as a tampon in a cadaver.

—Ech, you c'n out-gross the eight.

—I thought you *liked* images drawn from medicine. Isn't that what your little poems were all about? Something has to explain our little "marital breakdown" beyond *your* mid-life crisis. There are couples around here, you know, who *have* stayed together—despite everything having blown to hell—or haven't you noticed?

—Oh, sure: Mr. and Mrs. Parkinson—the prematurely aged—clinging to each other, hangin' from each other's arms to keep the boogeymen away...

—eight boogeymen, to be exact—and I'm looking at the saddest of the bunch! Oh yes, you're too "youthful" to settle for a "senior couple" fate. Anyway, why don't you just leave? We've had this argument too many times, as well as the one about how you just need Something More out of life—God knows, you never were willing to let *me* go for more: no, those fancy fertility investigations were more than you could bear. No, not for you... Yet here you are, making your snide remarks to me about not wanting to wake the children... You bastard...

—You through?

—Matter of fact, I'm not. Because it seems to me that because we didn't keep going with all those fancy infertility procedures, we just naturally *assumed* that the miscarriages were *my* fault, me who had "the more active sexual past," as you never tired of reminding me, while *you, poor you,* sat up all night studying medicine—though it seems that lately you've been making up for lost time...

—Here we go again, 'round and 'round...

—Now, of course papa galloway tells even the young folks that their child-rearing days are over, that they're all too fried to even contemplate the idea. Yet, there are rumors going around that a child has been born to two young townies, who's absolutely normal...

—Sounds like a John Gideon Christmas special...

—galloway's warnings won't stop couples from doing what comes natural. Even if they're firing blanks. But what was that word you just used—*fried*?

—A manner of speech. What I'm saying is, it still hurts every time you rub it in that we couldn't have kids—though, had we managed to, I'd have been stuck raising them myself...Being a father wouldn't have kept you from your latest adventures...You *knew* about my pelvic problems before you married me, so why would anyone who *wanted* children have tied the knot with someone like me, with my history of "pelvic inflammatory disease?"

—At the time I wanted *you*—not children...I figured there'd be other ways to wind up bein' more than just two lines in the *General Practitioner Times*. And speaking of making my mark, let me tell you about one right-eventful thing that happened since we were last together.

—If it's dangerous I don't want to hear about it.

—What's *not* dangerous?

—As long as it's not another woman, like you-know-who—*plural*.

—You never believe that things at Carla's or ma's aren't like that; they're strictly playful—harmless flirtin'. You know, *pre*-genital. But *listen up*: today, I actually had a run-in with cabana.

—cabana...

—It was incredible. Never mind exactly what over, but...

—I can guess. One of the town women knocked on my door and told me.

—What did she say?

—That you up and lectured the entire town, that galloway invited you to smooth things over, and that you wound up shootin' up "some puhfeckly decent people."

—It was self-defense; I jest grazed 'em...

—It's always self-defense with you...

—Is that *all* she said?

—That's all; what do you expect from a townie? She did well to get that much out.

—There's more to it than you can imagine...

—Like maybe how you were lyin' aroun' scared inside ma's while cabana's fireworks display tied Will Gordon into a knot and drove him to kill himself...

—I feel sick about that. But you know so much—you do all right for someone who never leaves the house.

henry pulls her close.

—henry, I *figured* you weren't directly part of that tragedy. I may call you the world's worst sell-out. But I know that what happened unsettled you. You're not a complete monster—not yet, anyway.

—Claire, I keep hearin' these demonic cricket sounds at night whenever I'm alone—

—Tell me. Tell me about them.

—I already told you. But what I really want you to know is this: I looked him straight in the eye.

—You mean the *c*-word, or Bill Gordon?

It would've been hard, looking Gordon in the eye. —No, I meant cabana. I stared him in the eye and I answered the truth—after the town-hall meeting—when he asked me where I'd been. I just *told* him —Ah been at the town-hall meetin', cab. I sensed that even though that's what he *figured* I'd been doin', even though it was the worst possible thing to have *been doin'*—as a member of the eight—it was also the only thing I could say that he'd accept; it's like I sensed he'd respect my *honesty* or somethin'.

—And did he "respect" you? She mocks, intrigued despite herself.

—The strangest thing. He just smiled and went on with his card game.

—Deep guy, this cabana. Some wonder if it even *has* vocal cords. So now you're all proud-like, being respected by this paragon of decency and respectability—

—Give it a rest...

—No, you give it a rest. You may have as much guts as brains; I'll admit that. But I have to marvel at the kind of grouch appeal this cabana packs. I mean, you're supposed to be *honored* if he shoots a warning your way… But before you head out to celebrate your little *tryst* with the beast, let me remind you that cabana is probably etching your name on a bullet this very minute—to be delivered, no doubt, in a more discreet location than Carla's saloon.

—You know, Claire, I couldn't care less. I'm ashamed at the tingling I feel when I remember the actual words cabana said to me…

—It *spoke* to you? It actually speaks?

—You *are* impressed. Actually, what I *meant* was the words *I* said to *him*: I was at the town-hall meetin', cab. But he did come very close to speaking—he nearly said —Where ya been, henry?

—*Pro*-fucking-*found*.

—Just about, but not quite. Why I'll bet the other seven wouldn't have believed their ears had he up and said the words.

—You know, Henry Morganstern, I wish I could recall what I once saw in you. The kind of achievements that *used* to make you proud. This showdown stuff is just so, so unworthy…

—Claire, you sure you've been taking the medicine galloway gives you?

—Never miss a dose. She shows him a faint ski trail of red tracks on her forearms. Pulls down her eyelids. —I been vapin' too. Though he switched me to a higher CBD to THC ratio, for total body relaxation. Makes the time between shots much longer.

—Well you'd better not miss out. It's important if you're to keep on…

—…without crackin' up?

—You have been missing doses, haven't you?!

—No more than you miss punctuation marks or capitals when ya talk, sugah. Not many. But I guess you don't need me pressing all your conscience buttons at once, now do you? Wouldn't you rather keep riding your Claire instead of riding with the eight? She slaps her thigh.

He pulls her towards him for a kiss. But she pushes him away.

—Claire, I swear that after what happened to little Gary, and to his poor dad, and then that good-intentions fiasco at the town hall, I was gonna walk away from it all. Maybe ask you to take me back.

—Okay, henry, so that's how you *really* felt. So, please, honey, do me a favor: leave. Don't keep looking me up just to tell me we can't go on meeting like this. You can't ricochet off me like a bullet just to get your strength up. I get awfully ticked being your rock, henry morgan.

—You're fed up. Course you are. But we're not just star-crossed; there's a curse on us of another kind. When I walk into that saloon and the coldest piece of AI that ever passed for a man gives me an order—or a glance that somehow conveys an order—then I realize I'm not what you call the old Dr. Henry Morganstern. Never did like that name. It was too *something*.

He goes on: —And I don't have two grams of the old intellectual balls I used to—I've become a part, not as willing a part as galloway, maybe, but just a part of the way things are around here.

She touches his forehead, a big tear rolling down. Quick kiss, forehead then lips. But as she leans into him, he pulls himself a bit back, pressin' his groin into her side but with his face turned away. Snaps up his gun belt, draws a deep breath, and it's surface time again as he says —G'night, then. By the way, what ya doin' for sex these days?

—Why at forty-five mr. morgan—Ah'm quite content with thawed carrots, mebbe an unripe banana or two, plastic, o'course, like everythin' aroun' here...now that I had to use the old sex toys as candles. And you...?

—Doughnuts—'bout the cheapest thing you can purchase by the dozen. galloway's bottomless larder holds boxes on boxes of frozen Krispy Kremes.

—Mmmm, do get me some. Gives her little belly a rub. Oh, aren't we just the dirtiest pair of old marrieds around?

—Certainly the flirtiest. Night, Hillary.

—Night, Bill.

—God help us through this. I sound like John Gideon, that self-made son of God.

How courtship slides silently into the morass of married life: from trusted to crusty.

—Goodnight, she answers and takes to cryin' some on the couch. So much in love still, she resolves to search through his boxed belongin's first thing in the mornin'—remind herself who he really was before this bad dream swallowed them both. But her lips tremble as she walks to the mirror and sees how much paler she's become—no doubt galloway's needles and pills are partly to blame for that. Realizes she'll have to stop takin' The Shots if she's ever to find her old henry again—or her former gen-you-whine self.

REVELATIONS

carla writes a letter

It's howlin' out, one of galloway's dust storms programmed on the simulator—the storm track packin' an unfamiliar whistle an' punch combi-nation, courtesy of the shuffle feature. The big ones have left behind their usual mess o' whiskey an' beer bottles an' torn playin' cards. Couple townies come by to pick up some boxes of empties, wounded ones with blood soaked through their bandages. With things bein' kicked around in the wind outside, one of the eight offers t'take Carla home, kind o' serve as her big escort, but she jest smiles her feline smile, kind o' purrs —No thanks, boys. She bundles little Lucy in the old blanket the girl uses as an overcoat—kissin' her real light on the forehead (which is see-through skin instead o' bone in some places) an' tells her —Thanks, honey. See you tomorrow. The unlovely Lucy heads into the ragin' night, tryin' t'keep her blanket from blowin' off an' thinkin' about anythin' to ease her mind off the God-awful cold and her fragile con-dition.

    Carla's all by her lonesome now, counters wiped and broken glass swept up. The chairs all tucked under and tomorrow's finger-foods removed from their dehydration packs for re-constitutin'. Though the wind's screamin' outside, there's a kind of eerie stillness inside 'cept for an occasional howl that pierces on through. Mebbe from some wind-chilled wolf cryin' and slobberin' for someone to let a singed-coat carnivore into their hearts—a soft-sell pitch to set up a peace of sorts and mebbe get a good meal if somebody falls for it.

Carla walks to the big mirror over the bar, smoothin' her soft hair, rubs a bit o' mascara stain from under one eye and sets down with a writin' pad pulled from under the counter, pluckin' a pen she keeps in her garter. Gives it a little shake, bendin' over it slightly (them cone-shaped breasts comin' into view like a long-awaited shoreline) and takes t'writin' a letter to her girlfriend Sharon (a.k.a. Meg) that works another saloon somewhere out there mebbe fifty miles into the desert—who knows mebbe a hundred and fifty miles:

Ah bin wahnderin' jest how youse a'doin' so Ah feggered Ah'd git yo' down a few lahns—jest t'sort o' tell yo' how glad Ah am 'at youse is well an' enjoyin' your new job at the Sa-loon. Lak, Ah...

Can you *stand* it? Well, I can't. All right, so you play dumb to survive, to keep their paws off you (no mean feat), to keep bread on the table. But God, Sharon, what good is bread when you're half-sick to your stomach? What comfort is it to keep them off your body when you can feel their eyes *glued* to every part of you?

Want to know the latest "hit" around here: Carla's purr. Carla, as you know, is me. I never was quite up to fitting myself with a pet name like *Meg*—didn't want to risk exciting them even more, as in —What's yer reallll name, Mahhhrgarit? Mahhhr-gerie?

As it is, I'm Cahhhla. And Carla's purr is the sexy little throat-noise I'm expected to make while being coy. Have you puked yet? And get this: the one they call, and I kid you not, "fat-ass jake" (the small j and all other small letters around here are *de rigueur*; seems the heavier a dude you are, the smaller your letter—needless to say I get a capital *C*) well, the aforementioned fat-ass has developed a crush on yours truly, which, needless to say, does slightly less than make me crawl under the sheets and spank the monkey.

Sharon, it's so depressing! Maybe *demoralizing* is more accurate. I try to keep my spirits up—honest I do. I tell myself, —Arlene, remember who you *really* are, and what you *really* feel inside, but I swear, even my own name *Arlene*, even *Arlene Galloway*, is beginning to sound like it could be anybody's name. And my mom is no slouch either when it comes to changing her name back and forth. If only I could spend a little time with her alone, I wouldn't feel so in the dark and on my own.

Maybe I really *am* turning into Carla—I have nightmares that I already have, especially when this Carla identity is all that keeps me from ending up as a dead pile of flesh, or from resigning myself to a life among the townies, those folks with radiation readings right off the charts. Some of them have physical deformities out of *Ripley's Believe It or Not*. But for the most part, they're just weak and tired.

Sharon, I can't wait much longer for the big Rebuilding and Reunifying program uncle harold keeps promising. But I guess I shouldn't complain. When my shifts are done, I have a cozy enough little pad to come home to—something straight out of *Cosmo*. Though I never feel completely relaxed. I get creeped out and can't shake this paranoid feeling of being *watched*. Sometimes I swear I hear voices in the walls.

uncle keeps saying we will be re-united with the rest of the country, but that the whole process of reestablishing a communications network and decontamination could take *years*! Meanwhile, he's been ingenious enough to set up and operate this self-contained biosphere, so how can I doubt him?

It's a shame that our conversations have to be so one-sided, but I can understand that you have to keep your replies short, ole pen pal! Though it's kind of you to reply so quickly—I hardly have to wait after handing my letter to uncle harold. Sometimes, though, it starts to feel like a soliloquy at my end.

Look, misery loves company. I need to hear about what's going on at *your* saloon. I care about how you're coping, and I sure could use some helpful tips. But let me finish my list of laments before I ask some detailed questions about your situation. (I almost wrote "yore" out of habit...I swear, if uncle hadn't connected me up with someone like you, who is in a situation exactly like mine, I'd go bananas!) How long ago was it I had a TV and a computer in my bedroom and a smart phone that could actually connect with live people on the other end?

But I might as well start from the top and move downwards—don't worry, I'm not going to catalogue the entire "big eight" for you and tell you what it is about each of them that turns my stomach into a constant knot and my nervous system into a network of little misfires. Let me just say this: you cannot know, you cannot *fathom* the extent to which the head cock around here, cabana, virtually terrorizes this town. Even educated men like uncle harold seem so small whenever he appears. He'll parade his way in here, walking so straight you'd think he was dunked head to toe in cement, with shoulders that won't quit, and a bulge in the front of his pants I haven't seen since ballet class; I swear, Sharon, unless he's stuffing stockings in there, he is built larger than any man—make that animal—I have ever had the dubious pleasure of seeing. (And don't go reading this as enthusiasm—believe me, this is one girl whose heart does not go thump-thump just because twenty inches of flesh with hair at the base and a man stuck to it struts by.) If I do happen to notice what I call "The Bulge," it's because he wears it like a flag; if you ever want to do a thesis on phallic dominance in the human species, tell your friendly neighborhood anthropologist to set up shop down here, commit some anthropology.

Anyway, what I want to say is, despite my ability to roll my eyes about this hulk after he's left, I'm beginning to feel he has some kind of power over me. That steely gaze, the way that he twitches just an end of his thick waxed mustache (could it be a stick-on?) the tiniest bit when he gets annoyed—so slightly you have to watch closely to even notice it. The guy could teach a course in hypnotic suggestion! And the way he moves! I mean, okay, who am I to talk—my own ludicrous hip-wiggle-*cum*-sashay disqualifies me from poking fun at anything—but Jesus! You would not believe it; he moves like a two-hundred-pound tiger, with such a sudden spring to him, such a panther-like—I'd almost call it *grace* but that's usually applied to sacred things—that in a second he's pounced, and looking on can give you a heart attack in nothing-flat. To wind up *at the other end* of it...

Reading over these last lines I see I still have a bit of a sense of humor; thank goodness I have you to write to, Sharon...

One other thing—though I could go on about some pretty gory incidents that have been going on around here lately, I don't want to add to your burdens any more than my frazzled mind forces me to.

There is one recent discovery I've made that shows me that people are capable of being aroused even under a constant state of siege. Now I understand how the starving millions in the third world could still get mileage out of a dried-out clit. (Excuse my grossness; it's the local culture...) I actually am beginning to feel the old interest returning a bit down below, even if it feels more like a danger- than a pleasure-zone.

His name is henry morgan—excuse me, to us grown-ups, Henry Morgan, and he does seem like a genuine human male. He is exquisitely aged, though it's true that the lack of contrast around here dulls one's powers of discernment. Fact is, the only Young Ones around here that aren't complete mutants (a story in itself) ride with the (yuk!) big ones.

I've had a feeling that mister morgan might be different from the others for quite a while. But I never could be sure, if only because I have to provide enough lip-and-eye service to cabana whenever the eight are around—and avoid eye contact with anyone else. As it is, the "men" are happy I spend any time with them at all in cabana's presence. Also, since henry morgan (is that not the world's coolest name—it sounds so, so *swashbuckling*) is the strong, silent type, I have no real material in my file on him, so to speak. Yet just today, I checked him out, gave him a bit of a looksy, just fleeting enough that cabana would only kill *one* of us if he'd caught me. The way that I got around the small-*c*'s surveillance was to lean almost up to his ear as I gave mister morgan the eye. I think henry noticed, though I suspect he won't dare actually try to communicate with me so long as the main cyborg is within a mile of either of us.

Besides, whenever cabana is around I'm so bloody terrified for myself and for whoever else is talking to me or even looking at me that I'm relieved, no, *thrilled* when nothing happens. Really, it's turned me into quite the conservative, even at twenty. Not quite like uncle, though, who vows to go back to being a Republican as soon as we're linked back up with civilization. Maybe I'm just as afraid of change as a far-right Republican. I'm not really sure what gave me the sheer nerve to do what I did today—though a while back, on a day when I had really had it, I told the small-*c* something—something uncle harold had said—that I just knew might spark a confrontation. I just had to see *something* change around here, and I trusted that someone with as much high tech at his disposal as uncle would be able to manage the consequences.

Wait! I know what gave me the courage to make contact with morgan. *He* did! henry morgan stood up to cabana at one of the gambling tables today—that's right, and he's the first to do anything like that since we all ended up in this psychodrama. Strange, I almost forgot the whole thing—probably because I couldn't believe my own eyes. Which brings me 'round to another worry—the extent to which I'm turned on by morgan just because of his size or strength or some equally shallow dimension. I mean, with the likes of cabana and that scum-bucket ned hanging around, you hardly want to make strength alone your cry-terion for the ideal male—or you just might find yourself *impaled* on your own yardstick. I do wish that mister morgan would reveal himself to me somehow, give me something more substantial to go on...

Anyway, best that I leave off on this frustrating subject of love. There aren't many other candidates out here. Except for morgan, there isn't a man within miles I'd find more interesting than a warm shower, a quick finger-game and a cup of jasmine tea with a book to keep the old mind alive—unfortunately uncle's collection is a bit overly padded with tales of the Wild West—but have you read *Lonesome Dove* or *All the Pretty Horses*?

Well, tomorrow I'll try to keep a straight face when bloody willy (can you believe these names?) walks in, orders a rye and tonic then plunks a few sugar cubes into it—and I'll try to keep from vomiting when trapper dan, who's as close to a walking toilet as a "human bean" can be, decides to use his—I'll try to keep this letter cleaner—to stir his drink.

And maybe I'll try to force a smile the next time big ned—that Yosemite Sam on steroids—looks me up and down with his natural-born-killer eyes, as though he were sizing me up for a pine box or for bedroom plans that are no more wholesome—but oh God, things feel even worse than they usually do at closing time—

An' she looks up at big ned's bushy eyebrows 'n prominent glabellas amblin' her way.

She lets her pen glide to a stop and sets it gently down. And tries, an' jest tries mind you, to git up some kind o' smile. But big ned is lookin' meaner 'n crueler 'n more horrible than ever, his eyes red and his face all black with small balls of dirt hangin' from his mustache, his eyes gone completely range-hollow as he shows her a bushel full of teeth an' innard'ly growls.

—ned, why ned, what ARE you doin' here? *Goddamn it, Arlene, you've GOT to just smile now, smile and get back into character—pour him a whiskey—HE DOESN'T WANT TO HURT YOU—look now, he's grinning—a bizarre grin, but friendly? like a circus bear on K—just don't blow it—just put down the letter really slowly near the beer tap and—*

—Yo's is rattin' a LOVE lettuh, CAH-la? Thet raght? Har har har!

—Tee hee! *Goddamn, that's unconvincing—you're blowing it* —Wha, *yesss*, ned, *Ah izzz! Don't encourage him too much, for Chrissake* —Ah jest been gettin' down two or three letters to my—er, banker—if you wanna call THET writin' LUV letters, tee hee hee—O love letters in- in-in-d-DEED

No time to stammer...

—MEBBE YO' BEEN FEELIN' kind o' PRONE to doin' some lovin' lak, ain't thet pussy-ble CAHHH-LAHHH har har har. (With each laugh the bluish upper lip slips up to reveal a beefy red tongue lickin' each pointy canine—they's pretty well all canines—then flippin' back in so that the simpleton face gives way to a crueler version.) MEBBE YO's interested in lovin' IN GINIRAL...

HE'S COMING. TOWARDS ME. O GOD!

—Now, ned, *r-r-really...*

—DON' REALLY ME NUFFIN'!! he roars then softens an' says quite mattuh-o'-fackly —Cause Ah's been chasin' aftuh ghost-girls on da range fo' a long, long while (continues his advance) and as fo' yo' sweet little banker—if'n his name is GALLOWAY then Ah aims to MUDDAH him...

His temple veins take to bulgin' like ram's horns.

—ned, now we really, er, you really must... As he swipes for her she arches back against the mirrored wall—she's soaked, her hands clenched to small fists with the whole fear thing only firin' him up all the more.

—ned, what if CABANA comes in...

—He freezes. Like pourin' ice water on the head of a drunk. He jest freezes and looks at her real stupid-like—an orangutan strivin' t'answer the skill-testin' question—but he zeroes in his murder-glare as he considers his next move.

Carla/Arlene (Arla Carlene) reaches her hand back real-slow an' tries to pour him half a chilled draft to settle him while he's holdin' back. She knocks the glass to the floor—reaches for a second one alright and tries to control her tremblin' fingers under the tap. All the while watchin' his druggy eyes contemplatin' what ezackly to do with her breasts, whether or not to poke at 'em to see if they're attached or mebbe try an' turn 'em inside-out.

An' suddenly ned's thick sausage-fingers fumble fer the ripcords on his fly and the string gets longer 'n longer as it unwinds out the flyholes— ned snortin' 'n spittin' foam 'n bein' crazy in giniral while Carla is still up against the wall like a plumbline, tryin' to grab fer a bottle fer protection. An' ned's unwrapped a regular frenchbread o' himself, hairy with a great dorsal vein pulsin' up 'n down like a browny-red viper pointin' full-menace at her face as he bleats out *CAHHH-LUUH!!* He takes to pullin' it up and down, up and down, with Carla pressed against the pine—her eyes a couple of *O*'s now, an' ned just throws' his hairy ass in and out and continues his fireman routine with his throbpole now a cherry red, but he ain't approachin' further—jest starin' at the *V* of Carla's plunging neckline an' a pullin' at hisself in a frenzy. Soon he's sprayin' spume from his baboonal, thick wet gobs fricasseein' down his pants, jettin' out on the bar like mucilage and foam, 'til his wad is spent with Carla still tryin' not to pass out, blotches of ned's spunk on her outfit steamin' away—then in a second the bar doors swing open and in strides henry morgan.

—ned, this ain' no time t'be standin' there wid yore pants 'round yore ankles, wavin' Old Glory at a lady—'cuz cab is only a couple blocks away an' cummin' fast. He's been askin' all day about how long and how wide you is, an' dollars t'donuts he ain't enquirin' 'bout your wagafoo neither—so tuck yo'self back in and head fer yore cave.

ned's red as a lobster, but he don't want t'be dead as one—nor do he fancy the degree o' his present ex-posure, what with cab fast approachin', cab who could monogram his cock with bullets from a hundred yards away. He slides his pants up over his ape-ass an' fumbles out the back way, lookin' over his shoulder with a goodbye 'n *waren't-thet-somethin'-special-'tween-us* kind o' grin at Mizzy Cahhh-luh, his holsters rockin' two cradled gats like they too might go limp with satisfaction.

In shock and sleazophobia all she can do is sob on the counter—arm up over her eyes in fear, embarrassment 'n rage. She spots her letter—soaked through now—an' she crumples it and swipes it onto the floor behind the counter.

henry morgan approaches her, careful-like 'n says —Ah'm maghty sorry for one o' my fellow eight actin' so un-ginnelmanly Miz Cahluh. Ah reckon you could use a day off and a nice long shower.

Though desperate to wash herself off, she drums her fingers on the counter 'n says —How *could* you!

—Miss, as Ah said, Ah AM sorry... But what the rest of the eight may or mayn't do is...

—*Stop it!* Cut the bullshit accent! An' she reaches into her lace bra and pulls out a small piece of paper. Quickly she unfolds it and hands it over—some kind of a list torn from a ledger book:

SURVIVORS ANNUITIES (h. galloway chief executor)

Halverson, Dr. William $50,000 per annum & lodging

Morganstern, Dr. Henry $50,000 per annum & lodging
(henceforth known as henry morgan)

Meyers, Arlene   business privileges, (saloon, lodging),
(henceforth known as Carla)

Seeton, Rose   business privileges
(henceforth known as ma rosemary)

Parkinson, Mr.   (for trap removal)
first rights to recycled metal and
$800 per month

And there's more and more names that in the quick flash of a minute are impossible to read. In fact, there were about fifty other names in with those that'd been *scratched out*.

But henry just gives her his big eyes, looks at her puffy red ones an' says —Ma'am, Ah'm afraid Ah nevuh was too good at readin'.

—You sonofabitch! And I thought you might be different! Not too good at reading, *doctor* morgan*stern*, you slimy old *Jew*.

She almost scores a rise with that one though henry cools down mighty quick.

—Phony, she presses. —Lookin' after your own hide to the bitter end... Interesting, how the last thing to disappear is the old ethnic identity. Or sensitivity about it.

henry winces, unconsciously touchin' his nose.

Which only makes Carla smile. And then for a second both look sad—morgan reddenin'.

—Look, she says gently, even darin' to reach for the arm of his buckskin jacket. —Pardon this stinking slime, she says, wiping it off with a towel and feeling sick. —I don't know how long we have to ourselves but I *need* some answers...

He takes her smooth hand off, places it gently back down on the bar, reaches for another couple towels. —Wipe yourself off. And remember: around here, curiosity kills.

—Come on, henry morgan—I'll still call you by your cool-dude name—don't you think I've put a few things together that I can't just sit on and ignore? It's dawned on me, for example, that I'm just about the only person in this town my age who's half-ways normal, that my "uncle" is someone with incredible power and, while I'm on the subject of him—why is my name down on this list as *Meyers?* I mean, that's a different last name from my mother's—which is down here as *Seeton*, when really, she dumped the names of all her partners and went back to her unmarried name of...

He deflects her: —Do you know the kind of trouble this note that you *ripped off* from gallo—from your "uncle" could get you into?

But Carla has recovered from the big ned show. She re-buttons her blouse and does what comes natural: fixes to pour them both a drink.

—Why, don't be so mo-rose, henry, dey ain't no danguh to dis note. Aftuh all, none o' you eight c'n even rea-ud. Or is it unca harold yo' is worried about?

—Maybe it's your "unca harold" *you* ought to worry about—his little goon-show's gettin' more precarious each day. Things are shapin' up worse 'n in *Westworld*. I mean, this big ned caper—I do admire you, Ar—er, Carla, for being able to compose yourself so quickly after *that*. You are one well-put-together young woman.

She looks at him in astonishment.

He finds his eyes rovin' and in embarrassment he pulls them back to his drink.

—Usually your magic works well enough to keep these goons in check. The fact that this brillo-bearded buffalo hauled out his firehose like that can hardly be seen as a sign things are gettin' safer...

Carla swallows with some difficulty. Plenty o' truth there. The awareness of it makes her lean towards the big, middle-aged man-of-the-world in buckskin.

—*Please!* A few answers! Just a few! Her young eyes sparkle through their own redness, even as a tear squeezes through, eyes so different from the lustreless eyes of his wife Claire languishin' at home. He feels like comfortin' her, almost hears himself sayin', *Ask, I'll answer anythin'*, but instead he gives her arm a gentle squeeze and says —Got t'go now ma'am, it's medicine time.

—Damn it. That was one of my questions. *Doctor Morganstern, what* is *this medicine that uncle gives out like vitamins? It's got to have something to do with why everyone is so apathetic, so subservient—*

—Hmmm, you's good with words, Miz Cah-luh. He finds himself reachin' over to plant a kiss just to the side of her eye, right in front of one of her little scrimshaw sailboat earrings pokin' out from within her dampened hair. —When it comes to unca harold's all-available designer "medicine," *Nobody* Does It Better. Scrinches his nose. —You go git that shower...

She calls after him: —I can persuade you, henry, to tell me more. 'Specially if you keep returning time after time to that burned-out, middle-aged wife of yours. I can offer a bit more *inducement* than she can.

To which he answers over his shoulder: —Don't you dare diss my wife—she's a Survivor. I'm surprised your nosi—er your curiosity hasn't led you to try a bit of your uncle's intravenous brew. Now *there's* inducement worth dyin' for...

—Wait! Two questions... just two.

—Cain't answer neither...

—First. How did we end up in this spaghetti Western? I know there was a disaster. It must have been something nuclear...

—Yep, unclear war, I calls it. Second?

—Your wife—is her maiden name Meyers too? You know, I've always felt, psychologically, that ma rosemary is my mother—but there's more than a passing resemblance to—

Well, one got my Botox treatments and t'other turned up her nose at 'em —*and now looks like a gran'ma.* 'Stead he says —You've been readin' too many of uncle galloway's detective books. He swings open the saloon doors, not knowing whether to curse her gumption or admire it—half-regrettin' that intelligence runs in families. An' that when it comes to survivin', intelligence jest might be a fatal mutation.

a relic

Before sunrise Claire makes her way through the empty street, carryin' the grams of BC bud that galloway had given her, a tiny hole in the crook of her arm still slowly weepin' into the cotton ball he taped on it. —This is a cop-out, she'd pro-tested, but he jest smiled and even dared to stroke her cheek—she should mention that to henry—then told her —This helps all God's children forget.

Is it some form of cocaine cocktail? henry once implied it was and that only he and galloway use the "nosey route," or could it be that concoction called ecstasy or perhaps a psychiatric drug with an ever-so-slight-but-definite after-buzz? Whatever it is, no sooner is it in than you have your Perspective back; Vitamin P galloway called it 'cause somebody, many bodies, had Blown It All (no fault of galloway's truth be told) and now what was left to do was, in galloway's words, Play It Out—galloway was almost as fond of card game metaphors as he was of sports talk and Wild West lingo.

Play It Out. She has to admit, windin' through the maze of alleyways that first unsettled but now bored her, that she does feel played out.

This morning as she unlocks her front door and sees the half-eaten croissant and crumbs on the kitchen table, she grows weary despite the lift of the meds—tired even of the treasure trove of frozen and dehydrated "gourmet rations" that galloway distributed so generously. True once the drug is on board she no longer wishes herself dead—as a matter of fact she's inclined to feel agreeable, almost grateful towards harold that this particular batch of forty-fivers was worthy enough to inherit the last days of human life on earth, that not only had they headed for the right place at the worst of all possible times, but they had done the only thing and therefore the best thing that there was to do and were therefore blessed as Noah himself. In went the drug and *This was It*, This was All There Was and by cracky *It Would HAVE to Do*.

But this mornin' she feels restless enough to snoop—with the help of the key she'd seen henry hide away after their last romp together. She'd pretended to be asleep as he was at the little desk he still kept for himself. Might he keep a journal? She doubts it. All she saw him put into the fireproof strong-box was a single scrap of paper. Was he still writin' poems? She shudders at the thought. *Poems about what? The joy of selling out?*

Even as she fiddles with the key, tryin' to get the heavy strong-box open, she feels strange—knowin' she's taking a risk, but unsure exactly what that risk is. Stumblin' on truths that might make it even harder to pretend? What might such a dirty little truth be? That papa galloway had had some part in endin' civilization as we knew it? Not *too* likely, mere champion of commerce that he was. That one of the many eggs that was removed from her years ago, to be mixed with her husband's sperms inside some other woman's womb—that one of them actually *took*, but no one bothered to *tell* her? That she really does have a child out there—how often she has turned to that little fantasy for sustenance. henry's repetitive taunts seem to point that way too.

The whole infertility work-up had been her idea—henry criticized what he called the medicalization of the birth process, though he had never agreed to adopt, havin' seen too many couples inherit "other people's problems." She's glad she'd forced him to go through all the procedures with her. It meant that some life-giving part of her might still be out there somewhere. What would it be like to have a son or a daughter? Maybe a daughter like that lovely little hussy Carla, to whom she could teach the ways of the world?

Not exactly immortality, but it keeps hope alive.

If there is a risk it is tied up with Henry Morganstern, the young doctor she had married, and in a kind of way has stayed married to even though his soul—*their* souls are being eroded down to jokes about a lost profession, lost religion, lost values. What was *lost* rather than any quest for meaning is what draws Claire to snoop this morning. She has to risk it—though she can see through the window that the treeless street is already softly lit by dome light and it will soon be daytime. At the beginning of the day she told herself, *Today I take a chance*. It made her feel something like the old unpredictable excitement, the kind that wasn't brought on by medication.

As she lifts the heavy lid of the box, she comes upon a relic. At the very top of all the papers, most of which are piled in folders, is the single sheet henry had locked away the other night. It is a poem, one of the few she actually remembers—he'd always been reluctant to read her his poems aloud. Not that she's a fan of poetry—certainly not the modern stuff that didn't even rhyme. The poem has a medical theme too, so he had either been a medical student when he wrote it or was just starting out in practice. It's astonishin' to come up with something in this cartoon republic that actually has a meaningful past. She lies down on the carpet and reads.

A Poem About the Pancreas

Even if you set up your practice
on Harley Street
no patient will come in with complaints
about his pancreas:
"I think it's my pancreas, Doc!"
—unless he too is a fellow professional,
also educated

out of his natural mind; few patients
will even be alarmed by the word—how unlike
"the heart"
a word that means "the biscuit"
to the best of us.

Years from now
when you trundle in
thin and yellow, depressed,
for abdominal films,
you too will have forgotten
your pancreas, and the news "It's cancer
of the pancreas." will hit
like an old family secret you knew all along;
"I'm sorry, but it's cancer
of the sweetbread."
"Not the sweetbread."—"Yes,
and, with proper medical management,
early surgery
and a very rigid diet,
you can look forward to
another six months"; when the pancreas goes,
it goes.

Those among us who are diabetic,
whom the pancreas torments
by degrees,
cannot describe this Familiar; even a poet
is at a loss for a metaphor.
Nothing short of a surgical exploration
will unearth
the thick spongy worm
buried deep in the viscera,

silent behind its curtain of peritoneum,
—with a head, a body
and a tail,
using the man's face.

She puts the poem down and takes a deep breath. Here is her serious Henry again, a man who is above using tits-and-ass humor, the poet-turned-doctor she had known and loved. She too is feeling jaundiced and depressed—and pained by her own lack of body tone. She begins to shake as a terror creeps in—the drugs are no longer holding, no longer keeping terror at bay. Though it has been years now and there is a new policy—of alternating drug weeks with sleep weeks—to prevent tolerance from developing. She reminds herself that it is nothing but sentiment—that sentiment and nostalgia are the *real* enemies. Wasn't it henry's *victory* over his soft side that allowed him to adapt here?

Yet look at her. Even the words *Harley Street* make her ache. She remembers the Jeffrey Archer and Agatha Christie detective novels she once enjoyed. The idea that there might be nothing left of Europe is almost enough to kill her. She can only pray that maybe there is still something left on the other side of that ocean—if there still is an ocean—if only to keep sacred the places where she and Henry had gone on their honeymoon. But she can hear galloway's wisecrack—that whoever still sings "There'll Always Be an England" hasn't kept up with nuclear physics. She can hear him joke that the only thing left of Western civilization is its number one discontent—that *he'll* show them *Western* civilization with a difference.

She recalls how Henry used to always worry about the enemy *within*—how he'd develop every symptom in the book whenever he studied a new organ system in medical school. —Claire, you wouldn't believe it—there are a million ways the body can go wrong! Mine, yours—

While now, the only threats seem to be the ones that stalk you in the streets outside—the young ones, the undrugged ones, the ones who have no history, no loyalties, whose flimsy self-control depends on the improvizing of their coach and controller—their very own benevolent family friend—harold galloway.

To her surprise, she finds herself replacin' the poem in its box, just the way she'd found it. She wants to turn it over in her mind some more over a hot coffee—wake herself up some and fight the party line on what now is reality. But as she lays the poem down, the top edge of a sheet peeps out from the thick folder just beneath it. In it most of henry's dusty writings are stacked in a thick pile. The last word of what looks like a title is the word *Elephants* and it makes her choose the poem from the folder. It isn't one she's seen before. The full title is "A Cosmology for Captive Elephants." She notices from its date that it was written just about the time the two of them were investigatin' their infertility.

A Cosmology for Captive Elephants

> Don't count him in
> on any herd activities;
> he's a solitaire, belongs inside
> a cage of logs, chained to a diamond-shaped rock.
> And when the slow cows saunter past
> they don't even look at him,
> sashaying in their wrinkled house skins,
> their young reaching for their teats,
> each with the support of five other females
> should he bash his way through
> for a moment of freedom.
> But what would such a moment
> bring down on him?
>
> Can he approach all six at once?
> And what will the feeders and handlers think:
> this bull no longer fears or respects man,
> this bull has forgotten the sacred word, "*Crush.*"

Even the food pellets we feed him
make him restless
when he should be
content.

What kind of life is this, I ask,
watching the night pass,
my wife beside me, so deep in her pregnancy
that I am left worrying for two.
I try to wake back to the world,
to tell her that the new cosmology is Fear,
but she rolls over massively
with a drawling "Goodnight, Hon—"

supportive, if entirely asleep.
So I ease back into my pen
of silence and Valium,
my tusks going soft, losing air,
my trunk curled up
like a toy.

That *sonofabitch*! A "solitaire" indeed! So that's how he felt about the prospect of her becomin' pregnant! *Even while* accompanying her to the clinic to have air blown into her fallopian tubes and large-bore needles sunk into her belly.

Somethin' more disturbs her about the poem: it feels like it was written by someone who *already had* the experience of raising children or at least of havin' a pregnant wife. She begins to wonder about this—though the thought of it makes her sick. She knows after all that henry had been married once, before they tied the knot together—a loveless marriage that only lasted three years—to a very wealthy young woman who had never managed to free herself from her father and his millions. This woman had moved back to New York soon after they separated and never looked henry up again. Could this have been by mutual agreement? Might they have had a baby together, who went with the mother as part of some kind of separation agreement? What if henry *had* fathered *and* abandoned a child of his own? After all, he'd been pretty cavalier about making all those paid-by-the-shot sperm donations in medical school. What if he'd even got himself a vasectomy some time after his divorce? Is he that much of a psychopath? To have not told her yet subjected her to all those invasive tests? A vasectomy would explain why he never really insisted on birth control—even though he hadn't been keen on having kids—and why there was no way *he* was going to "submit" to any kind of "male infertility work-up." She can't quite manage to put such knavery past him—he who now rides with the eight, albeit with all the right excuses.

She goes back to Pandora's box, fumbling with the latch, and snatches a third poem, which is shorter.

A Marriage with Children

A marriage with children is worth
the endless procession
of meal after meal,
imperceptible segments
of the gigantic flesh-colored worm,
...the need to think about food,
to cut and slice and re-warm
then eat while you feed
and clean up while you supervise
the child's play of others; and then
the need to plan the next meal...

makes the biggest meal yet
of your leisure time.
For that's what family
feeds on.

Him and his "leisure time!" She'll show him leisure time! She snatches a pile of other poems and squeezes them into a tight ball. In her other hand, she sweeps up a vial of pills and heads to the bathroom to pop them all. Well maybe half—no point killin' herself and provin' to him that only struttin' cocks can cut it in the brave new world. Yes, why not plug into harold galloway's virtual reality one more time, cooperate with the thick goo already movin' through her veins—a potion to try and overcome this new bitterness seepin' down from her heart clear on down to her toes. No point in becomin' distraught about what is no more—even less point frettin' about what might have been—this marriage with children that her good yuppie-doctor husband had so looked forward to.

She should be no more concerned about her lost marriage than she is about—her pancreas! But just then, she turns to find a stray page that had escaped her angry gesture. It landed face up. She remembers the lovely time she and Henry had enjoyed in Montreal, and their visit to this unlikely museum of living things.

At the Biodome

At the Montreal Biodome
a dozen codfish, each with three dorsal fins
and a homely barblet under the chin,
wind their way behind glass,
beneath the steely gaze
of a prehistoric sturgeon.
How fair a sight to a fisherman
should hordes of such grayish-brown fish
once again sluice from an opened net
onto the brine-slick deck of a ship.

On the fringe of the student ghetto,
on her birthday, my far-off daughter got "nudged" by a taxi cab
that nearly knocked her under, then sped away

—nothing like a friend's son,
who, wearing headphones as he crossed a busy street,
was killed by an SUV
a block away from the Montreal Biodome.

Children are as plentiful as the cod were,
ubiquitous as bullets,
of which every minute 30,000 more
are manufactured, along with five new guns to fire them.
Every minute someone falls to armed conflict
in a dark-skinned land
lacking a single home-grown munitions plant.

Next decade at the Biodome,
strange visitors will arrive
wearing faux fur and scales
to view the new endangered species:
a cautious optimist, perhaps a pair,
hiding out in the arboreal forest,
waiting for a sign that the age
of men hunting men has finally passed
and the world can be reclaimed
for the resolutely alive.

Is she still one of those? she wonders. Resolutely alive?

a visit to harold galloway

henry morgan gives a deliberately annoyin' shave-and-a-haircut knock on the heavy steel trapdoor of harold galloway's bunker—a door so thick that from inside it must sound more like a tip-tappin' sound. As always there is the obligatory three-minute wait while he is checked out on the monitor.

He turns his face upward and to the side to present an insistent and menacin' profile. He had socked back a few beer at ma's despite a little agreement with himself to always be the most sober cowpoke in the saloon—a survival measure that usually comes easy given how prone he is to nasty hangovers. *Damn Judaic genes.*

He is finally admitted by galloway in robe and slippers. He can practic'lly smell the man's aftershave through the door.

—Oh it's just you, says Liz Claiborne tryin' to look Hugo Boss. —Give me a second while I switch off the surveillance.

Even though henry has been down here a hundred times he can scarcely believe his eyes. The peach lighting from the tinted pot lights bathes the sunken living room in a Palm Beach Worth Avenue glow so that you always look tanned. There are the paintings, several Rothkos and Jackson Pollock's early *Night Mist*, which henry had urged galloway to include in the memorial cache—these along with older museum pieces galloway had picked on his own on the basis of which were the most famous. If they're good enough for the curators...

Actual *house plants* thriving under fluorescent grow-lights. After all these years the ficus and schefflera still give off the deep green shine of life and light so strongly it could blind a man inured to the sagebrush and cactus outside the complex. True, a few hardy plant species that double as trees survive on the town streets—mainly locust trees like the ones that used to survive the pollution on busy city streets, but they look for the most part like anorectic girls. Only thick blades of coarse grass and faded dandelions can grow anywhere outside the dome, which makes galloway's hoard of livin' things all the more a miracle. Like Monsanto, he now owns the life forms. —It's all done with mirrors, he gloats with false modesty.

—So, mister morgan, to what do I owe this honor? He sounds distracted.

—Hiya, Zwyxy. Just here to gawk at your buried treasure.

—Have you come to insult me or merely to imbibe, as usual? Perhaps you'd rather visit later and return, for now, to the animal kingdom outside. galloway must have been lazin' around in his Zegna pyjamas *cum* bathrobe, watching *Casablanca*, which is still playin' on his antiquated DVD machine. He is in no mood for a visitor, especially one in need of humorin'.

He ignores the Zwyxy reference since he has no memory of his troubled childhood.

—Remember how we kids concocted that Zwyx Wyhollymer nickname for you? henry taunts. —As far back as third grade we called you Zwyxy cause a group of us agreed you were such a bottom-feeder you deserved a nickname made up of the very last letters of the alphabet. Remember? Course, you were a couple years older than me and in fifth grade—which is the only reason I allowed you the honor of trailing after me and my fellow third-graders... No one your own age would have you.

—I choose to forget the past, thank you. Unlike you, I *outgrew* it, *surpassed* it. As for being a bottom-feeder, mister morgan, aren't you the one who goes to ballet performances and makes sophisticated remarks, such as: —The men in the ballet are the ones with the asses? galloway turns his back to morgan and flicks the remote control to his old-fashioned Blu-ray machine—playing the same image on screen as the ancient Toshiba HD. galloway pumps up the volume of Bogart and Bergman's eager voices to transport back into his movie. Now and then the image fades or the actors' words cut out due to generator surges. With his eyes still on the screen he adds blandly —Your Zwyx has come pretty far in life, don't you think?

—Ya figure? challenges morgan, humorless.

—Yeah. A bit farther, I might add, than the rest of that same "Pride of '59" who are, by now, I should think quite thoroughly incinerated...

—*Bastard!!* henry lunges at him and—despite a little twistaway motion by galloway—soon has him tangled up in his entertainment system wires, his large bowl of popcorn knocked over on the rug. —I'll wipe that smug little smirk off your face.

—You *crazy?!* I didn't do the incinerating! Lighten up! *I didn't take the goddamn fish out of the ocean!*

henry's knees dig into galloway's softly padded arms as he savors pinnin' this magnate of high finance like some oversized bug. —It may not have been you Zwyxy, but it was your *kind*! The least you could do is have a little...

—The *least* I could do is exactly what you've been doing, morgan! *I* do *plenty* around here. Now, get *off* me!

—Tell me what the power source is!

—God, God alone is the power source! Ask John Gideon—

—Don't fuck with me, aphid!

—What d'you care what the power source is? Let me be! Do *you* want to supervise a small cadre of townies in a machine shop? Dull, deadly dull, I assure you. They work on their own; they're like the Morlocks in *The Time Machine*.

—*What is it?* Turbines on an underground river? A portable nuke reactor? What does the grand power cable connect to? Ans'er me!

—It could connect to my ruby-red asshole for all you need know.

There's a pocket reactor—DARPA came up with it, there are two back-ups, and *everything, but everything's,* encrypted to the max. Now let me *be*!

morgan lets the bug crawl free. He throws down the gauntlet —It's your contempt for human values that produced this B-movie world—and you're gonna pay for it.

—So that *what*—so *you* can run things around here? Fat chance.

henry isn't up for runnin' much. More eager to dish out retribution than to actually try to change things. What's the point? Ever since retiring from the thoughtful medical life, he's ceased being a details man. No drudgin' in galloway's technosphere for him.

—For God's sake that was *buttered* popcorn, you galoot—what a mess... Let me remind you, morgan, that this country elected a B-movie star who super-saturated the world with nukes, and then eventually followed him with a dyslexic governor cowboy with a back-firing missile shield. Then came a two-term bi-racial prez—followed by an ass-ass-ination and the new Republican clown-prez. *Those* class acts went a long way towards hastening the end. So for fuck's sake: *Don't Take It Out On Me!* Why not just get nostalgic and watch a movie with shots of the World Trade Center? Then maybe you can make the switch to the present tense. You hopeless romantic...

morgan flops into the plush couch that forms two sides of the sunken living room, looks down at the exhausted galloway nursin' mighty sore arms and surveyin' an Exxon Valdez of a popcorn spill. A genuine BP Gulfer.

—Relax, galloway, it's not crude oil... Remember *that* stuff, all the grief it caused...? Remember Hiroshima—Chernobyl—Fuk-you-shima?

—I suppose you think I can pull a rug-cleaning company out of my hat too.

—You could pull one out of your ass, I'm sure. You know, harold, I remember our days together in elementary school—mygod we go back a ways...

—Don't remind me, says galloway, reachin' for the remote. —I'm in no mood for this...

—Yup, you were just another unpopular fat kid, about as poor as my own dad was, and we were bussed up to that snooty little parochial school from our working-class neighborhood. Yup—designated gifted.

—Finished?

—Not at all. I remember the two of us in the boys' washroom of Richview Elementary. We had both gone in to take a leak, but you decided, with only a few minutes left to recess, that you had to take a crap—and you asked me to stand guard for you.

—What on earth would compel you to remember such a detail—other than a generous dash of the latent homosexuality we've come to suspect in you, dear friend and poet-without-tights, *master* henry bates?

—I don't know what made me think of it now—maybe because of that gorgeous marble-tile bathroom over there, with the ferns and the Jacuzzi; it's mighty enticing, goddamn, even has its own little hot-light so you don't get your snivellin' little round-shouldered bawd too cold when you come out of the shower.

—The ferns, I regret, are artificial silk. False as a woman's love. But your *point*?

—Well, when I looked into that bathroom just now, I had that memory of me standing outside that little aluminum stall at Richview Elementary while you jest plopped and stank away— it was truly rich.

—Your *point*, Gutterstern.

—I remember thinking: I have never before experienced a more awful smell—I mean, it was an *omen*. Even back then you were *totally* anal—why, all you ever wanted out of life was to make a million dollars.

—Well morgan, as they say, if you seek a glorious peninsula, look around you... Let me put on a strong pot of coffee. Best thing to cut through an attack of nostalgia.

—Single malt Scotch'll do. Make it your best...

—The single malt's for *friends*—like myself: how about some cognac, VSOP?

—Very Special Old Person, like y'rself.

galloway uneasy. —*If*, of course, you're willing to accept a drink from a pariah whose excrement smells like mine. I'm sure with your steady diet of beans and bread *yours* must smell like *roses*—no pun intended. But you are in a scrappy mood today aren't you? Or should that be tonight? I lose track of time down here. He yawns and nods at the dawn simulator on a timer. Feigning boredom, he heads for his fold-down bar. Made of curved wrought iron in the shape of an elephant's rear, it allows him to survey his stock. —I see I'm going to have to work harder at re-programming—keeping you solidly *on side* so to speak.

—Is there another side around here to play for? asks henry, toein' patterns in the thick rose Oriental rug with his cowboy boot. —Oh, by the way, sorry about decoratin' that bit of rug over there... I want to kill you, not trash our—er, your—mementos.

—That's my boy, back to your senses; I knew you still had some basic civility. And galloway hands him a snifter with a couple ounces of Courvoisier swimmin' 'round, the *Casablanca* machine unplugged from one of the fat wires to the generator. He collapses onto the smaller love seat across from the sofa done in the same floral pattern.

—Fact is I need one of your lectures again to remind me that *There Is No Choice*—or not much of one—so that I don't have to feel tortured every time I look at that beautiful young woman I fathered—who suspects more than she ought to. When she looks up at me with those hazel eyes—of *mine*—I tell you she'd slay me even if she weren't the only young thing around here...

—First delete the "father" reference; you are not *pater*, you are *progenitor*. I once heard this sperm-bank director say that to a bunch of prospective sperm donors when they got wide-eyed about the idea of spreading their seed around the world. Besides, Car—er—Arlene, or whatever you *prefer* we call her, was raised *neither* by you *nor* your good wife...

—But by *your* good sister rosemary—and now you get to pose as her loving uncle harold...

—Spare me the sentiment, henry. With all my professional activities, I haven't had time to develop a true father-daughter relationship—not even uncle-niece, for that matter. With "ma" Rose there *has* been more of a connection—thank goodness. It's why she's turned out as well as she has. Though Rose's ex, Sam Seeton, didn't stick around very much longer than the child's first year, as you'll recall. Then there was good ole Sam Meyers—your Claire's cousin—who, unbeknownst to him was raising a blood relative. Well, *he* didn't stick around more than a few years either... My sister always did have an edge to her when it came to men. And just look at the dudes she has to deal with now... Ha, it's precious!

—Oh, yes, "ma" rosemary, indeed. Puts on that sweet-but-frank Kate Hepburn shit, but in actuality she couldn't wear a miniskirt on accoun' o' her balls would show. Maggie Thatcher revisited.

galloway suppresses a smile. —With all the snooping we've been up to, it wouldn't have done well for me to have gotten *too* close to my so-called niece... Though let me tell you, henry, I have plenty of sweet, sweating young things on DVD over there courtesy of Mr. Andrew Blake—and we're not talking tasteless here—that'd make you forget that little "daughter" of yours. galloway makin' little quotation mark flicks with his fingers in an immensely faggy way.

henry leans forward to spring again, considers chuckin' his brandy glass at galloway's graying head.

—*Whoa*, henry, *Whooaa*! Relax! yelps galloway, pudgy fists hidin' his face then grabbing at his achin' arms. —Sure you're still sensitive about availing yourself to some sights of your own flesh and blood—and I admit, I *conned you* into watching. But you must admit that Arlene does seem to stir more of that yummy fetish stuff in you than your own wife does—isn't that so? You know you're middle-aged when firm, youthful beauty stirs up feelings of awe more than lust. She is rather awesome. Look, I got you to profane your biological tie with her for a reason: she'll be less able to lure you into doing anything stupid—I admit that. You're not likely to think of her as your daughter anymore, are you? And wouldn't she wind up being the first mental casualty if our little cover ever *did* get blown—

henry hands his glass to galloway for refuelin' and looks down at the floor. —You know that our little Arlene somehow got her hands on *a list* that has my full name on it, as well as the name of her second step-father Meyers? A list that spells out the sordid details of your various payouts to us local upstarts. And that her last name on said list reads *Meyers*, not *Galloway*? Your sister ma Rose's last name is down as Seeton.

galloway grows thoughtful. —So she knows she's not my niece—or that *maybe* she's not. And that Rose isn't her biological mother... Well, we'll just have to fill her in on all the various divorces her dear old "mother" has been through...

—You never cease to amaze me, galloway, how you can tell a lie without breaking mental stride.

—Practice, henry, practice.

—But don't you think our Carla-fied Arlene is going to be more than a tad interested in knowing who her *real* father is—in the biological sense...

—Of course she will. But I'll just give her the old time-tested psychobabble about being her "psychological" parent, and I'll brief Rose as best as I can about what to tell and what not to tell...which I admit may take some thinking... But tell me, henry, how could she have gotten her lovely little hands on such a list? How did *you* find out about it? How much of our ruse did you reveal to our comely miss?

—Look you! Show some respect for my daughter...

—Yes, yes...

—And the rightful daughter of my lawfully wedded wife...

—Spare me, henry! No one forced you to hand over your wife's precious little eggs to my sister—someone who was a *hell of a lot* more prepared, mind you, to bring children into this world than *either* you or Claire were: Claire was pretty heavily into the booze and dope by that point, was she not? *Desperate Housewives* style. It's just as well the conception took place in a more hospitable, if somewhat more mature uterus.

—Claire went through *three* miscarriages, jerk-off, before I handed over her reproductive rights to you. I got sick of it, sick and tired of the whole thing. She took each one of them harder than the last. Stopped our sex life dead in its tracks.

—Three miscarriages and precious little support from a workaholic husband... Besides if it wasn't for my ability to procure a little lead-lined existence for her still-developing brain, Arlene would never have turned out to be the perfect species of young woman she is.

To which henry can do nothing but grab the arm of the sofa and push himself back a bit—his boots now up on the rosewood coffee table.

—How about a little respect for the furniture, mister morgan? You're not at ma's. I can't just dial up a handyman.

He lowers his feet.

—I told Carla nothing—not a thing. Course, she's wise to the accents—how could she not be? And she's figured out that, unlike most of the eight, I actually have mental contents—and more than a few extra years on them. I've tried to toe the official party line. I think my old buddy in academia Mr. Amos Barton has also played his part convincingly enough. But what a tangled web...

—Less tangled than the web that led to this, I'll remind you! Terror, terror, counter-terror. *Ka-Boom.* Homeland Ministry, Homeland mystery: homeland misery... The US launchin' retaliatory nukes only compounded the damage.

—Sometimes these damn drugs of yours cloud me so much I'm not sure I believe that story.

—But I've got the ending *on film,* remember? At least the complete destruction of the area around here—if you'd care to sit through it again... Sorry there's no audio track.

—Christ, to see your world ending *on film*—this *can't* be—it's so sick...

—Sick, yes, but satisfying. Bearing witness... They all laughed at Nixon for wanting his every word and deed recorded for posterity, at how his vanity did him in. Yet the Pentagon and NSA under Reagan then Bush then Bubba Willy then Shrub then the Big O then his GOP-flop successor filmed our undoing every bit as zealously. These bunkers that we locked the pooh-bahs out of have shatter-proof lens portholes in them so that the shockwave and thermal pulse were captured *before* the lenses got distorted by the meltdown. Yes, in the end the entire US did a double-Bush atop a Reagan.

—You keep blaming that fogey Reagan even though he left office years before the Event? Even though *you've* always voted Republican.

—Well, perhaps it is a tad unfair for the producer of a B-Western to blame a B-movie actor for paving the way... But remember how many *years* of treaty after treaty it took before the world could get itself back to just having no more nukes than it had *before* that man came to power. Even *that* number was ludicrous; remember how nukes would fall out of those rickety B-52's right over the Southwestern states, how only a catch in the fail-safe prevented them from going off *then*... Soviet nuke subs coming *this close* to a meltdown... The Gipper was a nuclear litterbug. And it didn't get much better under the prezzes that followed him. 'Specially the mogul with the nest on his head we can't allow ourselves to mention.

—True 'nough. But who are you to talk, jackass—you've gone 'n booby-trapped these sorry remains of civilization.

—You're not accusing me of arming dick-tators, are you? That would really be a departure, for an American to arm dick-tators. The Shah, Saddam, Osama, Gaddafi, Mubarak, Musharraf, the Saudi Royals, the Emirates, we could go on and on...

—Well, you can keep your state secrets—as soon as I can come up with some advantage to telling Car—er, Arlene the truth about what-all's gone down around here, I aim to do just that.

—Ahhh, "come up with some advantage," henry, how very *gallowayan* of you to qualify it that way. That you're still after advantage makes me suspect you're less than fully committed to capital-*t* Truth; it's the sign of a mature thinker.

galloway presses on: —You're not holier than *moi, mister* morgan. And if I can interrupt your paternal zeal for a moment, I'll remind you that you and Claire were emotionally divorced around the time she put the hit on you to start reproducing your kind. You were playing the field by then, as I recall... And it only took you one weekend to decide to forego the privileges of becoming a dada. Why, you should be thankful that my sister Rose had the good sense to join us here and bring Arlene along with her—that you still get to observe just *how superbly she turned out*.

—One more fuckin' comment *out of you*—

—*Easy boy, easy! Whoaaa!!* That's what you *heard*—not how I meant it! Now you just set right back down again and pour y'self another strong one. Fact is, it really can't be said *whose* daughter Arlene is, given she was raised not only by Rose but by a series of nannies who helped Rose and a fairly brisk rotation of father figures, among whom yours truly is just the latest. Besides, even if I concede you biological paternity, I'll remind you that you used to donate a lot of sperm to the local bank—at what was it, twenty bucks a shot? So you might be the father of *all kinds* of handsome and beautiful things who were once out there, who have now pre-deceased you.

galloway continues: —Just be glad one of your offspring ended up in the shelter I set up for myself *and* acquaintances—ungrateful though they've turned out to be—a biosphere *cum* bunker system Hitler would've marveled at. Consider yourself lucky I was eminent enough to have commandeered what was originally designed as a strikeproof Valhalla for the last of our godforsaken missiles.

—And looking back on it, I did quite a number on the Pentagon, securing the dome for myself, especially once the confusion of the final hours set in... Imagine them wasting precious minutes trying to decide which branch of al-Qaeda or ISIS delivered that first salvo of nukes out o' Pakistan. For all we know they came from the Chinese—or Russian mafia types that got their hands on illicit "tactical nukes." Ha! "tactical nukes!" Turn the world into a carcass, but do it with tact! But not to worry, we answered them all in kind—even while they were en route—bombed the shit out o' 'em, back to the Stone Age as President Nest-head used to brag.

—So what if our little strategic missile defense wasn't worth Jack. But you have to hand it to those fund-o'-mentalists—who would have ever thought of dusting off the old *kamikaze* phenomenon: more plane crashes than take-offs! More truck-bombs than trucks. Concrete barriers a staple of every courthouse, every mall. Why, all those two-bit domestic terrorist *poseurs*, with their anthrax, smallpox and plague scares. We developed such a case of The Cooties we plum forgot about all those wayward foreign nukes. Who could keep count of them? What with sixty Hiroshimas plumbing the deep on a single nuclear submarine. Why, Shrub couldn't even get the word right: *nucular*. Me, I always called it what it was: *unclear war*. The Pentagon top brass liked that.

—You pick a carcass like a jackal, you know that?

—Oh my—damn me with faint praise, why don't you?

—Why the fuck don't I...

—The secret is all in the lack of commitment—as in the martial arts, henry, my boy—commit too much weight to one leg, and *bingo*—you get thrown.

—And you? You've committed to this little goon-show. And you're dipping into your own shit. I see you sneaking rails—that constant nasal drip of yours ain't the common cold...

—Yes, well... around here it's pretty common... the air quality issue we have would hardly allow me to choose cigarettes as our universal drug, now would it? Unless they were made of candy or chocolate. So we'll have to all make due with booze and all the prescription drugs our hearts desire and brains can stand. Besides, henry, one shouldn't confuse a sensible thing like drug abuse with the kind of commitments that *really* weaken legs—like "falling in love" and the like; now *those* toxins I steer clear of!

—I'll say you do.

—Or religion, *there's* another. Why, the world's major religions backed policies that could only be called mentally defective. I'm not just talking about the religions of the swarthier cultures of old. Look at the Catholics—with their planetary-suicide laws against birth control and abortion. Seven billion earthlings and counting... Sewing ideas into po' folks' minds that condoms didn't really work against AIDS. Mind you, I admit that as soon as them Moslems and Hindus and whatever else migrated to North America, they got sane pretty quickly—except for the ones who trained in our flight schools so as to learn how to blow us up and crop dust us with bugs. And a few of them did do quite a number on Europe. But most of them were decent chaps—regular wogs. When there's money to make, people smarten up, they focus less on their holy books and fancy costumes and more on their business lives. Until they tilted t'wards global terrorism. Destroying capital. All *that's* bad for business...

—You say *business lives* the same way most people way *sex lives* or *love lives*. Business, that's *your* religion galloway—

—Guilty as charged, *Doctor* Botox... You know, it's only your past good head about finances that lets me tolerate you; your flowery side has always been grating. I'm an old WASP. You're a middle-aged Jew. Once those two kinds of people are freed of their respective churches, there's absolutely no difference between them—absolutely none, provided, that is, they hang on to their good business sense. They can sit back in the company boardroom with each other over a cognac, especially after they were allowed into the locker rooms of each other's country clubs.

—I love your Keep It Simple social analysis.

—Had you remained stuck in your adolescent "poyet" phase—you know, like when you were a young medical student touting *socialism*, of all things—well at *that* point you wouldn't have been worth saving.

—*Saving!* You call *this* being *saved!*

—Oh, my apologies, Jews don't take to being saved, now do they?

henry sets his glass on the table and considers tearing galloway's throat out of his head—but starts to feel wobbly in the knees.

—Okay, I'll cut the Jew-baiting. Still, I observe that the *old* you would've hurled your snifter across the room, precious cargo and all; now you set down the liquid gold before you let fly.

—Cut the "pigs like us" routine, galloway...

—The bottom line, Doctor M., is that you lack the technology to turn things around here—though what on earth you'd turn it *to* is by no means clear. As an alternative, if you really don't like the little first-person shooter game we have going, there's always suicide, Will Gordon style.

Ah yes, the old taunt, galloway's favorite. Life's a bitch? Then die!

—Somehow when one has just sat through watching the world blow itself to shit, the notion of doing likewise is...

—Unappealing?

—Redundant. The old me would have said *abhorrent* and would've reminded you that there's not only suicide—there's also the possibility of *reform*.

—Oh my precious Reform Jew. Sorry, I can't resist... Yes, so you overthrow me and try to run your own Operation Noah...

—*Operation Noah!* Remind me, weird harold, why it is you chose *six* of one kind of animal--lettin' me and amos b. off the hook for a moment—and exactly what species *it* is s'posed to be?

—Ah, disowning our own hard-earned membership in the eight, are we? All the steroids, all the Viagra and Cialis you can pop...

—I reckon if somethin' happened to me, *you* could sub in pretty nicely and try a dual role around here—if it weren't for your weak knees, stiff neck and spinelessness in general... No get-it-up pill could help you, galloway.

galloway shrugs off the taunt. —You could run this little game of *Streetfighter cum Survivor* all by yourself, or perhaps with some duly elected townies—no doubt with liberal democratic principles to guide you. Even figure out what to do with the rest of the eight—but my, how quaint they seem when viewed from the comfort of a bunker...

—They're, okay, *we're* really quite the insurance policy for you, aren't we? A Might Makes Right society only you can control...

—Patterned after *what was here all along*. I remind you: remember armies, Mr. Gandhi? Remember Secret Services? Those whacko patriot and sovereign citizen groups, with their own militias, that got the newly minted head of Homeland Security to move in with us... How many civil liberties were there in the end, once your cherished notions of "privacy" and social welfare collapsed? And all it took was a few packets of RDX and HMX on a few well-chosen subway lines to soften us up for the main Event.

—Yup, I reckon you need the eight the way Maggie Thatcher needed her IRA, her Skinheads, her Argies—living proof that absolute authority is the only way, lest anarchy prevail.

　—Pro-fucken-*found*, as a great man once said. Anyway, in *my* little world, it's IQ not physical strength that ultimately makes right. Which is one of the reasons that you, and even that wife and daughter of yours, keep it interesting for me. Gives an added dimension, an extra wrinkle for me to have to deal with. Mind you, it always was an IQ aristocracy, the world we lived in. 'Til the cynics started stacking the government with know-nothings like Dubya who the Unca Dicks and Halliburtons and defense contractors and Pentagon and right-to-carry NRA could keep in their back pocket.

henry goes glassy-eyed. Politics'll do that.

　—You still there, *Doctor* Morganstern? The old henry would have wanted to get inside my head, maybe toss a few *psychological theories* my way—about my *unconscious* reasons for setting things up this way...

　—galloway, I doubt your type even has an unconscious—you're nothing if not deliberate, deliberate to th' core.

　—How about this: maybe I peopled this world with powerful goons in order to "replay a trauma"—a "clash between Superpowers"—like the one that I cannot *bear* remember and am therefore condemned to repeat, ha ha—Or should I use more high-tech language and say to "reboot," ha ha. You must admit that the possibility of big ned having it out with cabana—ohhh, who'd have dreamed that a little virtual reality could have produced such a pair of *super*-goons? Much more *immediate* than the Arabian camel or Russian bear or Chinese panda or the sheiks of Araby versus the balding American eagle.

Suddenly henry's eyes start at the sight of a plump cockroach shuffling across the plush carpet on its way to the kitchen.

　—Shit, even *here*? Even *now*?

　—What do you *think*? We're under*ground*, aren't we? I'll have to put more of that edible brown goo out... Remember how the old doomsday books predicted they'd inherit the earth? They were right on that one. I mean, you've noticed just how lacking this town is in pregnant women... Seems every day Halverson is called for a miscarriage or "spontaneous abortion"; we just can't keep up with them. Just as well, imagine the doozies there'd be in a few generations, with more and more rads leaking in. It's amazing, though, that enough townies are still healthy enough to even *have* sex, given the radiation readings under *their* portion of God's little dome. Those get-em-up, keep-em-up drugs are true miracles.

—What are the latest readings? I feel nauseous some days...though it could be the company...

—Don't even ask—it'll only, how would your wifey put it—"depress" you. No, henry, you just go on living for today alongside ole papa harold, and I'll teach you a bit more of that high technology you always scoffed at—so maybe you can run this place when I'm gone...

—Ha! Someday my son this will all be yours—thanks a heap o' shit, pa.

—Well, I can always hand over my mantle to cabana.

—Ah, the old roaches-inherit-the-earth scenario.

—It's roaches in the end, no matter who takes over. And, don't get romantic ideas about the "the last of the normals" procreating or anything like that. Remember the blood lines and how funny your kids would be, with all them recessive conditions 'n all...

—A meeting of young and old, that really threatens you, doesn't it?

—I know I'm dealing with an old romantic; almost romantic enough to *do* that to some poor unsuspecting future-generation babe. Well, henry, papa harold saved *you* from Armageddon, if not from a fate worse than death—you might be stupid enough to try and do the same for someone else. Restrict yourself to attacking that relatively well-preserved middle-aged wife of yours—and reserve your daughter for spontaneous live visuals.

—*Bastard!* This time he does let the snifter fly—galloway ducking it like a batter at a plate, wincing as it smashes on the mahogany mantelpiece, rocking a fine colonial wall clock. But henry doesn't pounce again. Sees himself too clearly to follow through.

—My, oh my, aren't you *authentic*, mister morgan? You love truth even more than strong drink. Or hate me more than you love strong drink. Once again you misread me. All I meant is: stay away from her because she's our last form of jade-proof entertainment around here—I'm getting pretty tired of Les Femmes Erotiques, aren't you? Even the nude blonde on the beach sequence I've watched a million times.

—That's no nude blonde on a beach, philistine! That's a naked woman rising from the sea. She helped re-define "spume."

—Oh such a sad romantic, henry morgan. I'm trying to remind you that our last bit of Livent will last only 'til you blow *our* cover by telling her or anyone else about the local *Who's Who*...

—And what do you think your sister Rose—excuse me "ma" would have to say, if she ever found out about the little no-pay-per-view we have going here?

—You really want to foment panic don't you? Maybe she'd try to stir up the *golems* around here, just to defeat me. She always did resent "male privilege." It's been delicious, saddling her with the hairiest beasties this side of Tibet and watching her struggle in a sordid light-housekeeping arrangement...

—Revenge is sweet...ain't it Zwyxy? henry stands and heads for the trapdoor, looking over his shoulder. —Pardon if I don't offer to clean up...

—It would be out of character—your new character, that is. Just don't be surprised if next time you knock, you are not admitted. No matter what the radiation readings are. He then pushes a luminous green button and morgan exits into the anteroom. Watchin' morgan's back on a little TV screen, galloway buzzes him out of the plush lead-lined bunker, both men losin' their unlikely conversation partners, as they've resentfully come to view each other.

galloway switches his movie back on and stares, presses the mute button. As worried as bored. Bored with the "little girl and her baby" ruse that he'd sent ned out to chase; nearly bored with the all-look-and-no-touch guileless displays of the supple-limbed Carla through his wall of one-way-mirror—young Carla always did look a tiny bit like morgan, somethin' that bothered galloway and could interfere with his pleasure. For a moment he is even bored with havin' to escape the living monsters he knows are in hot pursuit.

He heads for the kitchen cabinet to open a fresh bottle of water, causin' an early-warning alert to go off among five or six roaches meetin' around a pool of spilled popcorn, antennae wavin' like rotifers.

Lookin' at the splinters of glass and the amber stain of brandy down his mantel, he reminds himself that Boredom Is the Enemy. He contemplates for a moment the needle tracks along his arms.

Thank goodness I'm back to the oral and nasal routes. I could always do the big S that I keep taunting morgan with, but in my case it would be murder-suicide. Who else around here has the know-how to keep things going? Luckily, my own dad, who had a healthier lifestyle than me, died well before sixty—that means just a few more years of this. And with tortured souls like henry and his progeny still walking on this last bit of synthetic earth, there's always a little sex-citement to be had.

Still, older sister Rose's snarky words kept repeating in his mind: convincing the US government to build a survival site *bigger than Biosphere* was an act of genius, but to have the compound designed with a Wild West theme—kind of The Pentagon Does Pixar—was an act of *comic* genius. Too bad about the rainforest biome packing it in so early, the outside air slowly leaking in.

Didn't you mean cosmic genius, dear sis?

He tears off a sheet from a dwindlin' stack of old office-memo stationery, barely yellowed these nearly twenty years, which still reads:

UNIVERSAL DEHYDRATORS

Harold Galloway, President

If You C'n Serve It,
We C'n Preserve It.
We Don't Waste
A Drop of Taste.

The motto that helped him win the good favors of vastly more powerful, if far less intelligent, men in the NSA and the Pentagon. Ah, yes, what a dry universe it turned out to be. He scribbles a quick note: *Boredom Is the Enemy.*

He grabs a dustpan and whiskbroom (one of those cute little sets where the handle of one fits plum into the handle of the other)—oh what *hadn't* he thought of rescuing from the past world—and begins sweeping up the bits of glass along the mantel. Checks the time on the wall clock. Still accurate. Then fishes through the pile of movies he'll be showing the eight tonight in the movie room: *Mad Max* and *Road Warrior*. Tomorrow *Terminator* and *Terminator II*. The final cauldron scene in T-2 says it all... Oh, an' the endless episodes of *Star Wars* and *Star Trek*...

There's a tear in his reel of *A Clockwork Orange*, the first half hour of which is just about right for tiny attention spans—'specially the part where Alex and his *droogs* wheedle their way into the home of an old *veck* and his *ptitsa, tolchock* the former while they *in-out* his wife before his very *glazzies* 'til both their *rots* are *creeching* with the *horror-show* ache of it all, *oh my brothers*... Thanks for that, brother Burgess. Those jockstraps worn outside the pants were the best.

The big ones would sit and watch for hours, guns safely checked at the door and ma sometimes dragged along as chaperone. *One day I'll run out of entertainment for them.* Ha—for *them*...

a chat in the larder

henry moseys in at midnight an' picks up a set of towels that a serene if worn-out ma hands him sayin' *Evenin' darlin'*. He never looks her straight in the eye. An' it ain't the same as his hesitation to look di-rectly at Carla when the rest of the eight are around. In that situation he worries one or both of 'em might crack a smile at the outrageous lack o'manners o' those he rides with these days.

He knows that even though ma's surrendered to her brother harold, she is—in galloway's own words—unbowed as ever. henry jest snaps up the towels, tips his Stetson and steps over some bodies dozin' in the clogg'd hallway. As usual the place stinks all the way through the Lysol moppin' it gets nightly, but cabana will be back in less than an hour, and so it's best that he bed down where he *ought* to be—'specially in these days of per-vasive suspicion.

He thinks to remark on ma's bein' up so late—on the personalized care 'n all—but best not rub it in. So he goes for a sleepin' bag, makin' sure there's no other body in it—livin' or dead—no scorpions neither. He does his five minutes of general toiletryin' before squirmin' out of his buckskins and insinuatin' himself into his bag like a wiener in a bun. His gun and holster hang next to the sleepin' bag from a bent-wood chair, and it's lucky he don't jump for them when he feels a hand on his shoulder gently shake him.

—Henry darlin', it's ma. Be a honey and help me out for jest a minute. Ah'm awe-fully sorry to wake you. Ah need a hand liftin' a case o' Red Bull out of the cold larder for tomorrow.

It's obvious why she don't try wakin' one of the more trigger-happy members of the eight, but that don't stop henry from grumblin' a bit as he pulls on his pants—ma havin' discreetly left the room to pry open the huge deadbolt on the steel larder door out back. It's dark an' cold, and more than once it's been used as a quiet room—to help one of the eight chill out for half an hour after blowin' their stack over somethin' or t'other.

ma in a night robe that's like a whole bunch of oven mitts stitched together, wearin' purple eyeshadow even though her gray hair is comin' undone, looks as drained as you might expect her to at this late hour.

—Funny time to fuss with drinks—ain't it ma?

—Well you know what they say cowboy—about a woman's work... ma opens the door to the enormous bone-chiller where galloway stores the next decade's worth of bottled, canned, boxed and de-hydrated food.

ma says —With your bare chest, in jest yore buckskins—why, you jest might catch yore death... Why don'cha tayke mah quilted robe, Ah have a flannel nightie underneath...

Needless to say he ain't takin' it... If one of the eight ever chanced upon him dressed like that there'd be a fairy-hangin' fo' sure. He also ain't in no hurry t'look over at ma in a state o' near-un-dress, though she can be a tad MILF-y in jest the right light.

—It'll only take a minute—you did say *one* case didn't ya? He steps in, gives a bit of a shiver, walks over and bends down to lift the case she'd pointed to—the proper way to lift, knees well bent 'n lower back nicely curved—and jest as he hoists it and gives her a "nothin'-to-it" grin he sees the door *closin' on him*.

He lets the case fall—*gassy bubbles to yore work*—an' hollers —What the heck maaa, c'n you hear me? his voice ringin' tinny in the con-fined space.

But the door is locked from the outside by a Schlage deadbolt. Suddenly it dawns: after all these years o' self-denying service—service perhaps in the name of savin' her adopted daughter Arlene and herself—ma Rosemary Seeton is every inch a galloway.

—*Rose! Open the goddamned door!* A joke is a joke! Ah ain't got no shirt on and Ah'm *frrreezinn' mah balls off...*

Loud and angry as his voice is, the voice that comes back through a little viewin' window in the steel door is deliberate an' measured. —Wait just a bit...cowboy, while Ah turn on the white noise machine in the dorm down the hall. Be back in a jiff.

Breakin' out in gooseflesh, he covers his chest with his bare hands. Doesn't dare yell much louder for fear of the sound carryin' through the larder walls to where the rest of the eight are cotton'd out.

—Very funny, Rose! I get it, I get it... Silence.

—*Look, whadda ya want?* Just tell me. So I can get outa here and head straight back to bed...with no r-r-recriminations.

—henry, dear. Are *you* in any shape to dictate terms to *me* right now?

—You *nuts*?! Do you know how *freezin'* cold it is in here? You want to *kill* me? Could you *live* with that?

—Hang on a minute, cowpoke, while I flip a coin. I've watched plenty of good folks die around here—the latest two of which were some townies I thought you were partial to.

Talkin' through her teeth like a fuckin' ventriloquist. Has to keep her voice down so they don't hear her. He considers puttin' his mouth to the window and screamin' loud as he can: —*cabaaa-nnnahhhh!!!* This is no time to plead his special case.

—*Cabaaa-nnnaaahhh!!!*

And she slides shut the little window, as it dawns: *She's trying to—is willing to—kill me.*

He knocks twice on the heavy metal—knocks mind you, not pounds—just so she knows he'll cooperate. No answer. He takes to doin' a few jumpin' jacks—keep the blood circulatin'—but bumps his head on a low beam. *God*-damn!

In a moment the crack to the outside world reappears. —You scream one more time, cowboy, *one more time,* and this window slides shut and *stays* closed *forever,* her voice clear and unnervin' in its calm.

—Spoken like a g-g-galloway, he grits through clackin' teeth despite his sore head, resentin' her use o' the word *cowboy* as a taunt. —*Waiitt!* Wait! I'm only *kidding*! Oh, *please don't close that little window again!*

—*Relax,* cowboy. There's plenty of air in there. Cold air, mind...

—*Please!* I'll die of—of h-h-hypothermia if you k-k-keep this up...

—Spoken like a former medic, she says. —Not to worry, henry, this larder ain't a *freezer*—though it's cold as desert night in there and then some. I reckon you could spend a night in it and still survive—least, if you keep active...

—*What do you want from me?* I'm not twenty-fuck'n-f-f-five any more.

—You're not? You mean you're near-f-f-fifty and maybe then-s-s-some, but you just *act* twenty-f-f-five? Or is it more like f-f-five?

Silence.

—What do I want? What *do* I want? I don't know any more, henry; I keep asking myself that. Maybe I'm just tired of waiting for the real Dr. Henry Morganstern to make an appearance.

—Just let me ou-ou-outa here and he'll return—s-s-sooner 'n you think!

Again the window closes. Its heavy slidin' metal gives a slight creak before it shifts shut. henry gives it all he has pushin' at that motherlode of a door, but it won't give.

He hugs and slaps at his arms and sides, his nose and mouth now dry and his lungs achin' with each breath. Knows that panic's only makin' things worse. But the pitch-blackness whenever she closes that window don't provide much encouragement.

It feels like a half hour before she slides it open it again. He jumps for the openin' —Th-th-think of what you'll do to C-C-Claire! Do you h-h-hate her *that* much!

—No, far from it. She used to be nothing but a druggie—but she's coming 'round...

—You think b-b-brother harold will let you get away with this?

—harold? *harold?* Why, I haven't heard you use that name in ages. Don't you mean "galloway," Mr. Morganstern? Or, what were some of those names you used to call him when he was just the unpopular fat kid in the class?

—Bitch, I'm not d-d-discussing fine points with you. Just let me out of this freezing hell-h-h-hole. I swear there'll be no—re-re-retaliation.

—*Freezing* hell hole, oxymoron, anyone? And my, look who got his letter *g*'s back. You are adaptable. Be back soon, henry—you just chill out. Maybe think about what going along with my brother has brought you. What pains me, henry, what's pained me all along, is how *happy* you seemed when the bombs started falling, how almost relieved you were to ditch your old life—patients and all. I always knew you and that wife of yours were never suited to be parents—or full-fledged adults.

—Oh, so *that's* why *you* were up for s-s-stealin' another w-w-woman's eggs. Fuckin' philanthropist! *Fuckin' barren bitch philanthropist!*

Again the window bites shut. henry resigns himself to sittin' on a case o' dry goods. Then tries doin' isometrics against a particularly heavy box. The intensity of his shiverin' is gettin' painful. He reckons he could crack ribs.

M-M-Maybe she really doesn't want to k-k-kill me. Though he knows she could do it—certainly from a practical point of view, no one but no one except Rose herself uses this particular larder, and it was very recently re-filled from galloway's central stores. But could she go through with it?

The prison window opens a trace.

—W-W-What about your *daughter*? You think you could live with *her* f-f-finding out that you *m-m-murdered* me?

—Don't you mean *our* daughter, henry? Oh, you are getting paternal in your sunset years, aren't you? Did you know that for the past while she's had the strangest feeling, like she was being *watched*? Why, in her own bedroom and bath... late at night, even in the morning...

—*That b-b-bastard b-b-brother of yours told you that!* Oh, this is r-r-rich! I don't believe...

—Aha, so it is the two of you who are violating her privacy! She told me she thought she'd heard voices through the mirror. Muffled, mind you... Lowest of the low, child-abuse low. I guessed she was right, but thought it too sick to believe. harold, on the other hand, well, we *know* harold's got people issues—why else would he have set up this goon-show? Anyway, henry, your low-down lewdness is strike two...

And again the window to freedom slides shut.

Baseball? galloway's always been a baseball freak—but his sister? galloway always drones on about man's inhumanity to man, about man's unwillingness to restrict his natural competitiveness to the playing field. *Because in life, as in baseball...* But a deeper shudder pushes through the shiverin': there are only three strikes in baseball.

Next time there's an openin' of the judgment day gate he's got the ice cream headache from hell. She tells him —Look at it on the bright side, henry, at least you'll be *well preserved*. Isn't that how you always describe me? A well-preserved woman?

—I p-p-promise, henry rasps. Anything—anything you w-w-want—J-j-just *n-n-name it*.

—Ah yes, Martin Luther in the lightning storm: save me, Lord, and I shall become a monk!

—Is that what you want Rose—for me to become a monk? I'll do it or anything else...*Just d-don't let me f-f-freeze to d-d-death*...j-j-just s-s-say the word...

But who can convince through chatterin' teeth? What a way to have to say your last words. —*S-S-Sadistic b-b-bitch! D-D-Dirty anti-S-S-Semite!* he hears himself leak out as the door makes things black again and henry morgan, like those in the endless line of losers who choke in the last innin' of the final game of the World Series—strikes out.

awakening

Henry Morgan wakes up in a bone-chilling sweat; he needs to vomit but cannot find the strength. What remaining strength he has goes towards pushing against an elephant sitting squarely on his chest, shifting its weight now and then to one of his arms, and sometimes his blurry eyes open to the gleaming white-tiled walls of the tiny infirmary. He doesn't need his *Merck Manual* to know that he's having The Big One.

The first person he opens his eyes to is Doc Halverson's nurse.

—You're going to be fine, if you rest for a few weeks. mister galloway sent Doc Halverson to inject you with an anti-clotting agent and something to keep your heart from speeding.

—How did I get here?

—You were carried here late last evening—about four or five in the morning—by black amos barton and ma.

black amos barton. Just as well. But ma...

—Who's taken my place in the eight?

—Townie kid, I'm not sure of his name; doesn't talk much, not many of them do. Now don't fret about that. Try to get some sleep. You're better off right where you are.

—Nurse.

—Yes, Mister Morgan?

—No visitors.

—Absolutely. You're about due for another injection for the pain. And, *please*. Keep those nasal prongs in—you still need the oxygen—that's probably why you're still in pain.

—galloway gas, he mumbles.

—I beg your pardon, Mr. Morgan? Or would you rather I call you Dr. *Morganstern*?

—Henry will do nicely...oh, and nurse...

—Yes?

—No galloways. I don't want to see galloways.

—There's more than one?

—No galloway and no ma rosemary. My requests should go straight to Doc Halverson. Ayeeeee ohoooo, I'm having a doozey pain now.

—That's because you're stirring up a hornet's nest. Just lie back, and let the heart monitor tell us what it can, and try to get some shut-eye. It took quite a while for us to revive you. We're not really a proper hospital here...

Heart attack. The great equalizer. The final proof that women really are superior. Just as he'd suspected all along: heart attack and stroke. 'Til they go off the rag and slowly catch up with us. He tries to turn his mind away from thoughts of Rose Seeton: but *how about* that ma rosemary? Didn't *she* turn out to be a piece o' live action! But such thoughts go straight to the heart.

For three days and nights there are no visitors. Just messages from Claire sayin' that Halverson has her on a gradual drug-withdrawal program—that by the time he is out of the infirmary, she'll be back on *her* feet too and off that bastard galloway's drugs.

On day four Sheila Gordon pays a visit, bringin' young Louise along with her—a youngster who would have been a smart-lookin' teenager, were it not for the sickly complexion shared by all kids of her vintage. The two have to wait outside Henry's room while he struggles with his bedpan—with the help of the nurse.

It seems a good ten minutes before he's able to see them. Sheila notices that Henry's breakfast tray of toast and jam and oatmeal has barely been touched.

—How you doing, Henry? Oh, sorry, this is Louise—she and her lovely little boy have become my new family. I've gone from being a mom to being a grandma.

—Pleased to meet you, miss, says Henry, a bit surprised that the young woman dressed in an attractive print dress doesn't blush or look away. In fact she seems remarkably confident—surprisingly so, since he imagined she'd be some kind of feral child when he first heard about her livin' out on range land outside galloway's dome. Maybe the radiation readin's outside the dome aren't as bad as galloway claims. Wouldn't that be funny? Stayin' put in whacko-land when you might just as well have left.

—Who's caring for baby? henry asks.

Sheila Gordon is impressed that Morgan has hung on to some social skills—despite his long sleepwalk with the eight.

The visit lasts ten or fifteen minutes—they don't want to tire him out. As they take their leave, Louise says —He sure don't look like one of those "big eight" guys. He's nicer. Sheila looks back over her shoulder, in a double-take. Dr. Henry Morganstern is looking every day of his fifty-plus years. A worn, distinguished look has taken the place of the rugged handsomeness. Strictly Gray Panther material. Must have been rinsing his hair all along.

As the older woman leaves with her adopted teen in tow, Henry notices that both of them have thinning hair in the back—even the younger girl, whose longer hair only emphasizes it. Louise also gives a cough that sounds as rattly as all the other kids'—like she's been smoking a pack a day for ten years.

One weekend night, Claire visits. Already she looks like she belongs in the land of the living—havin' put on a much needed ten or fifteen pounds. Would she stir up old resentments? Why bother with that now?

Claire knows better than to stay long.

Henry Morgan turns through a sheaf of poems Claire left with him—from what she calls his "journal." Much of it is his own writing, but among the papers is his favorite medical poem—a little-known piece by a poet who had attended a mitral valve surgery. James Kirkup's poem begins with a dedication:

A Correct Compassion

To Mr. Philip Allison, after watching him perform a mitral stenosis valvulotomy in the General Infirmary at Leeds.

How renewing it is to see these opening lines again:

Cleanly, sir, you went to the core of the matter.
Using the purest kind of wit, a balance of belief and art,
You with a curious nervous elegance laid bare
The root of life, and put your finger on its beating heart.

A balance of belief and art—he turns those words over in his mind for a while. Would his own sick heart rise again to such levels?

A garland of flowers unfurls across the painted flesh.
With quick precision the arterial forceps click.
Yellow threads are knotted with a simple flourish.
Transfused, the blood preserves its rose, though it is sick.

Some of the stanzas make him squeamish, odd` for a former medic. But he feels a curious thrill when he sees a couple of those old-friend perfect descriptions:

Now, in the firm hands that quiver with a careful strength.
Your knife feels through the heart's transparent skin; at first,
Inside the pericardium, slit down half its length,

> The heart, black-veined, swells like a fruit about to burst,
>
> But goes on beating, love's poignant image bleeding at the dart
> Of a more grievous passion, as a bird, dreaming of flight, sleeps on
> Within its leafy cage.—"It generally upsets the heart
> A bit, though not unduly, when I make the first injection."

The surgeon Mr. Philip Allison's prosy directives—set against the poetry—still hit home after all these years. Morgan speeds ahead to that final stanza, the one right after Mr. Allison's claim: "I do not stitch up the pericardium...

> ...It is not necessary." For this is imagination's other place,
> Where only necessary things are done, with the supreme and grave
> Dexterity that ignores technique: with proper grace
> Informing a correct compassion, that performs its love,
> and makes it live.

What necessary things still need doing in these remains—this ash-heap of a former world? How to rise to "a correct compassion"? Henry can only wonder as he looks up, only to see a new visitor materialize:
cabana.

Handsome as a nose-job neo-Nazi in a bulletproof vest, his wild starin' eyes burn like embers under a jet-black slash of uni-brow. Henry's heartbeat quickens as best it can, bringin' with it a burnin' pain. He thinks of Kirkup's heart, the stalwart heart somehow managin' to slog its way through a timely operation. For the very first time he really notices cabana's *age*. He can't be much over twenty, and mustachioed though he is, there is a telltale absence of age-lines to his horse's head of a face.

A refrain of the *Missa Luba* from *If* starts to pound in his head. He can see Malcolm McDowell training the machine gun on all the boardin' school's masters and student whips...

cabana smiles, 's if t'say —*Mohhnin', Henry.*

Swiftly cabana grabs for Henry's bedside glass and walks over to the sink to pour himself some lubrication, which he downs in a gulp. Broods back down again into the only chair in the room, at the foot of Henry's bed—knee of one bionic leg crossed over t'other.

In the lengthy silence Henry notices something else he never had before. cabana's ashen face is ridged and furrowed. Here and there are painful lookin' pebble-sized mounds. This young man has some pretty serious boils: —*Acne vulgaris*, Henry murmurs in a lament to no one in particular, and it comes out as a personal prayer.

cab shifts at this 'n draws a wiry hand across his face, almost self-consciously. Then he stands in a *Draw!* position, simian arms hoverin' above his holsters.

Henry just looks at him, as best he can. And in the most confident voice he's managed since before the larder fiasco, con-fides —I'm dead cab. I ain't never comin' back—never.

cabana seems to loosen up. Jest smiles a bit. Then he gits down into a bit of crouch and, holding his vice-grip gaze on Henry, he slowly eases the bedpan out from under the bed, lifts it eye-level to Henry like a sacred offerin' and gives it a splashy flick—the golden contents doin' a tidal wave onto the crisp white hospital linen. Then he flips the stainless steel receptacle upside-down on Henry's bed-sheeted lap before turnin' to amble out the door, not the slightest hint of frustration in his broad, young, but likely acne-ravaged back.

Henry waits in the stench of cold urine before callin' his nurse. Knowing she was layin' low 'til the departure of the visitin' dignitary.

Funny, I could've blown a hole straight through him had I kept a loaded gun under the bed sheet, the way I did the first two nights. But I was so out of it: who knows who I might have shot...

He had refused to let the nurse give him oxygen unless she let him keep his piece with him. But a couple of days ago he gave in, and she hung it up in its holster.

Why, next time I'll just call the po-lice...demand "more cops on the beat." He rings for the nurse who asks him on the PA if the coast is clear.

He thinks it likely is and asks her to bring him a pen and paper.

The thought of usin' his precious few remainin' bullets on harold galloway occurs to him.

RESOLUTION

an invitation

Henry c'n now sit up and is ready to take little walks 'round his bed. Why if this were a *real* hospital he'd be up in the corridors chattin' up other survivors by now: —We're lucky to still be here! Who's *your* doctor? and the like. He still looks awful—his color deathly pale, his teeth yellow with plaque and breath permanently sour. But he has plenty of time to mull over the locked-in-with-the-tuna debacle o' the larder. Why, if ma could only manage to get *all* her big boys to help her with a *real* big move, there's no tellin' *what* that li'l ole lady might accomplish.

He prepares for a proper visit with his drug-free wife. This time Claire looks painf'lly smart in a dress-suit he hasn't seen her wear in years. He resents her professional look as she strides into the room. The smell of Lysol permeates the air.

The sight of her husband lookin' every bit his age at first shocks her. He can see it in her eyes.

—I'd have come sooner, she says, kissin' him gently on the forehead, but I've had my own battles to fight, as you know...

—Don't treat me like I'm made of glass. He pulls her onto the bed and up against him—but leaves off mighty quick, and asks her to hand him a little plastic case of nitros. He breaks into a cold sweat.

—Phew! You're still some kisser! he tries makin' light. —But they always overheat these danged "hospital" rooms. Too bad galloway's Viagra pills don't mix with these nitros.

—I should leave. Maybe come back tomorrow when you're...

—Not a word. Just sit down in this chair. I'll be fine in a matter of seconds. These little pills work wonders.

He puts one under his tongue, then smiles. —With a marriage like ours, *one* of us ought to be poppin' something, no? Though lookin' at you, I would say you're on a *roll*...

She says nothing, just strokes his hand. —Henry, I need to talk with you about an offer I received just the other day, but seeing as how...

—Seeing as how the offer came from the self-same lady that put me here...

—How do you know that?

—Intuition. Why else would you look so guilty? Haven't found yerself a townie, have ya? Well, the nitro's working. Hop to it. What's the scoop? You and "ma" and Carla and who else, Sheila Gordon?—heretofore known as The Hens' Club. And weird harold, that ole rooster, he in on this too, or is his head also gonna roll?

—We're going to set fire to ma's—late enough so that they're all there at the same time. A certain conspirator, I won't say who, out of respect to your health—even told me that it was the desire to not harm *you* that prevented her from doing this before now.

Has Rose told Claire what she did to me? Too humiliating to ask her what she knows.

—So there's gonna be a big fire—you're just gonna bake 'em, eh? You gonna shake 'em first? Just like that? Then what? Have a bake sale? And papa harold—what's the answer to him?

—What do you mean? Who needs the bastard once we're free of his goons?

—Well, I don't know about that... You gals feeling up for managing a little high technology? Gettin' the generators to gen...? Tryin' to work with townies in the machine shop on a portable state-of-the-art nuke reactor of some kind?

—Henry, you know there are knowledgeable people around here; it's just that the town's men, and certainly the women, haven't had to use their brains in a while. They settled for demeaning Joe jobs instead. I mean, a man like Parkinson walking up and down the town, like a security guard—looking for booby-traps? He was trained as an engineer...

—Many years ago...and *not* on state-of-the-art survival—and surveillance—equipment.

—Look, Henry, don't try to snow us with the high-tech line. You yourself told me galloway is great at following the old K.I.S.S. motto—that things around here are no more complicated than a boy scouts' survival exercise.

Her use of the word *us* really grates. *How quick she fell in league with the evil Rose; sisterhood is powerful...*

—Boy scouts, hmmm—did I really tell you that? Well, even if I wasn't exaggerating, making this biosphere type of operation work requires a lot more training than any of these town guys has.

He didn't want to let on about the extent to which he himself had become galloway's understudy. *Let them work out their own solutions. Freedom should be earned.*

—I suppose it might be worth a try, he offers. —If you gals are up for a little *murder most foul...* But I'm not *entirely* sure that even Rose Seeton is up for actually *killing* her younger brother, and that's what you need to do to keep a snake down—cut off its head...

If she does know about ma's attempt on my life, she should own up now.

—I don't know about Rose and "her little brother," anyway. I doubt that killing him will be necessary. Since he heard what Rose did to you, harold has been depressed and brooding. We suspect he misses your company. Spends all day in his bunker, comes out only to service equipment and read dials. One benefit from all this is that the eight are a lot less hyper than they used to be; they spend more of their time lazing around, just eating, drinking and sleeping in late, like most punks do if you let them...

—I figured cabana looked a might subdued—for *him*.

—*He* came—*here*?

Henry doesn't want to go into that. It hurt to face the fact that his ridin' with the eight had been a source of energy to them. Somehow he'd never thought that he was really "goin' along" with them in that way. The idea that he helped legitimize them—even while galloway worried that Henry's joinin' the group might actually *weaken* it—makes him check out his tin of nitros again. His chest is still tight.

—What does any of this have to do with a turncoat-turned-convalescent like me?

—Well, we thought that you might set it up for galloway to visit with you...

—No.

—That way you could draw him away from his monitor screens long enough...

—No. N-O. As in capital-N-i-t-r-capital-O. Now hand me that little packet over there, please.

She gives him the medicine, stands, kisses him again, an annoyin'ly gentle kiss, the way you might kiss a letter goodbye before mailing it, says she'll be back in a day or two. Begs him to think it over. He wants to tell her he is proud to see her off the drugs and able to leave the house again... In a way he is proud of her. But he can't quite get himself to congratulate her. Let alone tell her how smart she looks.

Instead: —Any thought of my coming back to live with you—once I'm able to leave here?

—This isn't a good time to talk about that, Hen. We have to settle the issue of whose side you're on.

—I don't know, Claire, he says, feeling a new susceptibility to tears and bitin' on the inside of his lower lip. —I reckon the winner's...

Claire smiles, but rolls her eyes. —We're going to set things right around here, Henry, whether or not you join us.

She gives his hand a bit of a squeeze. —Of course, we so wish you would. And she too is out the door.

another visitor

Henry sets his pen down, half noddin' off from a poem he is workin' on called "Public Domain." He isn't sure of it—seems he's returnin' to conventional rhymes and rhythms. He remembers that phrase appearin' after traditional songs on old folk records, songs for which no writer claimed authorship, old chestnuts like "St. James Infirmary Blues" or "Come All Ye Fair and Tender Ladies." Reckons he's into thinkin' about public domains lately.

But first there's a piece of writin' he'd done that is now a nostalgia piece. These past few days he can't stop thinkin' of all those early girly videos galloway kept throwin' at him before he went hardcore. *Playboy* videos. From the days when the magazines still had nudies. He sets aside the half-written "Public Domain" to look over another piece, from an unbelievably long two weeks ago:

Playmate Playoffs!

Two teams of girls in bikinis, cherry reds
versus royal blues, sweating out paces
of unlikely water sports,
loosening, for the camera's lingering pan,

bikini-bottoms, windshield-wipering
as they saunter and prance, perfect
as body stockings.
Their assignment, to charge over barricades
but stay barely dressed,
milk-bodies creasing cutely, active bodies
surprisingly strong for such roundness
displayed as its own reward, like the tall blonde
who tugs at her bikini as she deflects off the barricade,
freeing her bottoms from the blushing grip—

I lean on fast-forward and stir Keystone-Kops visuals
—were ever goddesses put through such frenzied
paces by a mortal man?
Hef handpicks them for motherly bubs
with blending skin-tone nipples
and firm little choirboy bums.
No turning back from the search
for the right—expression.
But keep the sound off.
For they have the petulant voices of children,
make you feel like a brute
for listening in on the scripted fun.

The longer these plush athletes struggle
through their playoff feats,
the more languid the camera climb:
her drenched swimsuit bunching
to a thong she has to tug
into place—

Millions of men with nothing
they would rather do, no land

they would rather visit—but here,
where neither eiderdown
nor scrub-brush grows, where no lips
pulse or swell between the glistening legs,
only pale triangles into which California
disappears—

He remembers that after writin' it he had vowed to have nothin' more to do with galloway's erotica, let alone those shameful little live-action displays, the thought of which now sickens him as much as sleazoid San Pornando fare like *Anal Nation. Annihilation*, as John Gideon would put it. Those "adult" movies came wrapped in covers with fetching, beautifully lit photographs that gave no hint of the cold loveless meat parade inside. Respondin' to the threat of compulsory condom laws, the Industry threatened to move somewhere else. But it was all bluff. They needed the constant influx of would-be stars and starlets who, once desperate enough, would sell their nudity in exchange for more rent 'n gas money and a chance to keep chasin' their dreams.

Suddenly he hears from just outside his room a boomin' voice, a West Indies dialect: —Yo got ah leetle time for a veesit from a Beeg Black Mon?

—Name o' barton? he calls back, aware of the thin sound of his own voice. —Hold on a minute.

He slides the poems under his lunch tray. But one of the sheets of the *Playboy* poem wafts to the floor. —So long as you hold back a bit, amos. I can't let the old ticker run away on me.

In strides barton, salt 'n pepper beard an' his teeth flashin' whitely, extendin' a great big hand, the back of it so black it's almost blue.

—I'll pass on the handshake, thanks. I ain' givin' *you* a limp fish for a greetin'. Good to see you, amos. Many thanks for makin' sure I got here in one piece.

—What'd *I* do? asks barton, steppin' out of the fake islands accent. —Jest carried you like a sack of potatoes, then deposited you here—that ain't no day's work.

—Oh, I don't know, your back isn't that much younger than mine.

—No, shrugs barton, lookin' up at the acoustic tile ceilin'. —My heart neither... Those testosterone shots we get from galloway take a toll. You can tell *he* don't partake. They might help him break even.

—Well, sit down. It ain't against the law for a member of the eight to take a seat, is it?

—So long as it's not a back seat.

—Well, you ain't gonna be takin' no back seat to *this* here cowboy, 'specially now.

—You'll heal up. Then come lookin' for that little town mutant who replaced you—just another pock-faced kid, really, maybe *you'll* do a little shakey quent number on him?

—No, I'm done with that, amos, or should I call you Amos?

—black amos fer now. Stick to the plan.

—Okay, black amos. But it is good to hear you talkin' normal-like, it's been a long time... Why, you're almost like your pre-eight professional self. What was it you used to teach?

—Film theory, amos laughs. —Can you think of a crueler fate for a film-buff than to wind up in a cheesy Western? Why this ain't *The Wild Bunch*, let alone *High Noon*. Though *Blazin' Saddles* comes close. They both laugh.

—I c'n only stay for a bit. But let me ask you somethin'. What were you doin' wanderin' into that larder in the dead-middle of the night? ma was beside herself. barton looks at him real hard, like he wants, needs, the truth.

—Let's just say that ma and I had a "domestic dispute," and she ended up freezin' my assets. He nearly adds: don't do any errands for *her* in the middle of the night. But he passes on that, partly because he hasn't yet decided on Claire's invitation to join the conspiracy.

—I figured there was bad blood *somewhere*, barton answers. —ma never was much of an actress.

—amos, what if there were some kind of palace revolt—you know, to get rid of cab and ned and the rest of them. Would you be in?

—Ha! Palace revolt? Staged from "hospital headquarters," from this stinky bed? By the way, henry—you lose control o' yore bladder?

—Long story... No, but just suppose *someone* got some action going...

—You mean galloway?

—Well, suppose it weren't galloway. Suppose it was someone else...

—Townies?

—Jesus, just *suppose*, will you? Suppose you had to take on galloway? Henry figures he can ask it out loud; he'd spent the better part of an hour yesterday searching for hidden microphones—had found one and dismantled it. Whether there's some sort of closed-circuit television besides that, he can't really be sure. Let him lip-read...

—No, shrugs barton, I know what life would've been like outside this little shell lily-white harold set up for us. Had we not joined him—we'd be cinders, like the rest of our X-tended families. No, I dance with the one that brung me.

henry makes a little hand motion to barton—to assure him they're not being listened in on. But he won't come around. Suddenly, amos spots a sheet of typed paper lying on the floor and scoops it.

—Wait! You don't have to—

—Ho, ho! What's this, Henry? *Barely dressed milk-bodies creasing cutely...* This ain't half-bad...hmm, but what's this? You dirty old man, you...*freeing her bottoms from the blushing grip*...why, Henry, you could write for *Penthouse... Dear Penthouse*...ha! Now I never was big on poetry, but this I can relate to. Not your weirder shit. But what's this about: *firm little choirboy bums*? You have "issues," Henry?...pro-clivities?

barton backs off at Henry wincin' and holdin' his throat. Askin' fer nitros. He returns the page and says sorry, and gives his former mate a sound squeeze on the shoulder. He sits with Henry for a moment of silence before rising.

Leavin', he reaches into his vest pocket and pulls out a folded envelope that he hands Henry.

—So long, amos! God bless, Henry calls out after his friend's disappearin' cowboy boot.

a final pome

Henry is as embarrassed as one of the ass-letes caught in the relentless gaze of the poem. amos's leavin' helps bring his ticker back in line. Restores him to sinus rhythm, as Doc Halverson would say. He foregoes another nitro and gets back to workin' on the piece he'd started in the mornin'. It's different from the old *Playboy* poem, and he's burnin' to write it, chest pain or no...

For a moment he thinks of another literary type like himself—a former lawyer named "Slim" Reggie Canuck—now dwellin' among the townies, keepin' a low profile. Slim Reggie's hands and feet were de-formed by polio. Yet he c'n still accompany himself on guitar when he sings, and he sure does like to sing. For him, ridin' with the eight was never an option.

Slim Reggie liked to tease the good doctor about his versifyin'. He'd dabbled in the art but gave up writin' poetry early to try his hand at guitar pickin' and song writin' and even a bit o' journalism—what he called creative non-fiction. Initially Reggie pooh-poohed the flight to Wyomin' venture, having no more regard for Harold Galloway than Morganstern did—but once The World Situation began to deteriorate, he decided to come along fer the ride, takin' so many daily notes on the new set-up that he could give the Pickwick Club a run for their money. He got so into codifyin' the Wild West-speak that even Henry did some double-takes tryin' to git through it. Reggie said —*Somebody* has to pass along our story—if only for posteriors.

As galloway's intended bio-grapher, Reggie had the CEO's ear whenever he needed it. He was the only man galloway felt superior to, at least physic'lly. Reggie had more wit in his bent pickin' finger than galloway had in his sixty-string steel guitar, though he'd never say as much.

Henry closes his new poem with a wish, then mulls it over:

Public Domain
    for "Slim" Reggie

It's Pete Seeger bursting into banjo,
one more rousing refrain
from the Public Domain.

It's the right to shoot a man dead
and pay a rightful price;
It's camping out beneath the stars
without a job, between wars;
It's a Negro slave with a spiritual
and a crevassed face,
nodding over a bowl of gruel,
a cattleman high up on a gelding,
a steer at the end of his lasso,
a branding iron in place;
It's stringing wire and open fires,
routing redskins 'cross Monument Valley,
turn-of-the-century big city life
and violent death in the alley;
It's union men who sweat like sin
and die standing up for their rights,
farm boys pining for painted ladies

and coming to grief in fights.

It's everything our folks got through
to get where we are now;
Let's belt those pure folk song refrains
and make sure *it* don't gain on us.

He reviews it one last time: not bad for a first draft. Thumbnail sketch. But of what? Patriarchy? The word sticks in his craw. He remembers how he felt like a pussy-whipped dupe durin' his younger days in college, when he got roped into toeing the women's lib line. He'd gone along out of personal weakness and confusion compounded with anger at his personal patriarch—his father, who left him totally unprepared for the conventional male role. Until his early thirties he had to improvise and fumble around whenever it came to doing anything remotely handy. Nor did anyone ever show him his way around in a kitchen. *Thanks for nothing, Dad. Thanks too, Mom.*

Still, it speaks to things men have always been willing to die for, or kill for. He'll run it by Claire next time she drops by. But what he really wants—though God only knows why—is to show it to Rose.

He picks up the envelope barton handed him—pink with the initials H. M. on the front of it. He uses his pen to tear it open: in it are two slips of paper.

Dear Henry,

I meant to teach you a lesson, but *never dreamed* I'd nearly kill you. Please accept my apology for what you must be going through.

I hope you can see that I was willing to risk my own life by doing what I did. But I had to do *something* pretty drastic because your mid-life ride with the eight lent them a certain legitimacy. My brother harold knew it, and he counted on your cooperation.

I'd like to visit, but will only do so if you say the word, through either Claire or Arlene. I hope we can count on you in the difficult days ahead.

Wishing you a speedy recovery,
Rose Galloway Seeton, formerly known as "ma"

The other slip is simpler. It is another list, like the one his bio daughter Carla/Arlene had sprung on him, and it is in the same hand:

See reverse for encryption data for bunker, dome maintenance and DARPA reactor, including coordinates of machine shop location.
Just in case...

He isn't entirely sure *where* to tuck that one.

journal entry

Roses are red,
violets are blue.
Sick doctors must have
patience too.

Reduced to ditties. God knows, I can't write much else. Mornings are the worst. I get up after nights of sleep so light it's as if I'd never stopped thinking. By day my eyes are heavy and sore, my mouth has the foul taste of sleeplessness, pimples pop up on my back and face, and for the first time I have zero interest in sex. I also haven't had a crap in nearly a week—probably because I'm not eating. My thoughts turn over in slow motion, as if the groggy silt of sleeplessness were choking every last cell of my body.

    I left the hospital the same day they brought in Mr. Finlayson, a half-dead townie, formerly employed as a seam repairman who patrolled the dome and caulked the leaks. He must have had his job for too long, because by the time he was my roommate, his skin was covered in a rash and he had the worst case of radiation sickness I've ever seen—or heard, even for a townie. He spent hours with his head curled over a stainless steel bowl, vomiting and dry-heaving—not even galloway's IV brew could touch him.

Thoroughly nauseated myself from having to listen in, I made a decision: in medicalese, I "signed myself out" of hospital, and now here I am, at Claire's. But where *is* Claire? Out. Out meeting with Rose. (Ah, yes, roses are red indeed—they're absolutely livid.) She may even be meeting with Arlene—something she'd never have dreamed of doing before. And why is all this table-hopping suddenly possible? Why can three isolated womyn finally get together? Naturally, they've figured out *who each is* with respect to the other—there always was a resemblance between Claire and Arlene, even if they dismissed each other as junkie and painted hussy.

The possibility that Rose has told Arlene about her brother's and my past entertainment—*worse*—told *Claire*, makes me want to challenge Finlayson to an upchuck contest.

It's taken me half an hour to write this paltry journal entry. Not like I have anything else to do. My chest is still tight. I'm wearing a corset up to my throat, though the crushing chest pain is rare now; only comes when I "overdo it," to use Claire's little phrase for me tryin' to be half the man I used to be.

I never got around to saying how it is that the weird sisters now manage to hold meetings. You guessed it. New reformed policy by galloway. galloway, they say, is mellowing more each day. Rumor has it he might even be willing to "sponsor" his sister and her new friends in trying to change things around here—give up on his little divide-and-conquer imperium. They say he looks awful—looks his age, though more in the pink than yours truly. I still won't see him. The only company I have is Claire—when she's available—and Doc Halverson for check-ups; the old guy is annoyed with me for leaving the infirmary too soon, battery-pack Holter monitor and all, keeps urging me to leave this little *apartment* more—get some "exercise" wandering through the tubes around the town perimeter. He agrees that it wouldn't do for me to walk around *inside* the residential area, even when the eight (the new improved eight) aren't likely to be out moseying. Not that they'd shoot me dead on sight—they're out to thrill and chill more than kill, always were—though who knows: in my new reduced state I couldn't stare down a townie. And it would only take one o' them to make handy work of me if they got a chance. Won't even think what John Gideon could do. *Teddy Cruz ain't got nothin' on you...*

Maybe I *should* let galloway come over and lecture me. He might apologize for his sister's "appalling behavior"—that's galloway talk for you. But my keeping him away puts pressure on him to do the right thing, to take control over this jerky reel he's running. Before the bombs hit there were over 300 million guns in the hands of American *civilians*, more than 800 hate groups, and the Second Amendment trumped the sixth commandment. Not that I'm one to talk, with a two-gun holster still hanging on the doorknob... galloway hasn't yet seen the need to come get 'em.

Anything happens to me, Slim Reggie, and you get all this to re-cord. Someone has to work with paper.

film time

As the eight file into the dimly lit movie room, hangin' their holsters along with their greatcoats, only one thing is on harold galloway's mind: that once the *ladies* turn into killers—even would-be killers—things have gone too far. He'll show Morgan that there is room in this town for more than one man o' conscience.

cabana saunters in—always first to slide off his gun-belt, slowly turretin' 360 degrees before claimin' a front-row seat next to the popcorn machine. Watchin' that classic pecking-order strut, galloway starts to feel like the den-mother that he has turn'd into these past years.

It's not 'til the most madcap scene in *Mad Max* comes on that harold galloway gently closes the theater doors—oss-tensibly to block out that extra bit of light that might fade the film image, but really to start clearin' the coats an' pistols from the lobby. Though the feeble word *dis-armament* tastes bitter—makes a hideous bleepin' noise in his mind, like the word *liberal*—he nonetheless joins Schulberg, Doc Halverson, Parkinson, Abrams and Gideon as all five townsmen drag gun belts with Colts and Magnums and Smith 'n Wessons to the armory a good hundred yards away. It backs onto a gun shop—what's an American town without one?—*and* a liquor store, conveniently lo-cated in a slum where no one who counts for much will get hurt. With a heave-shut on a set of heavy, folding metal doors the gun shop disappears into the armory and both are effectively padlocked off limits. That simple.

Not that galloway noticed John Gideon slippin' on a particular semi-automatic Glock 19 of Tucson fame with a couple extra ammo clips under his gabardine vest. This more up-to-date modern weapon bein' an extra toy of cabana's—for years he's been allowed to keep it on him, 'specially since he's always the first to hang his holster.

A galloway more his old self would do a final weapons count, but he wants to get it over with quick as possible. With that in mind he hands each of his townie accomplices a revolver from his personal ko-llection. Each of the five guns chambers only two bullets. There will *have* to be some cooperatin'. After the recent town-hall meetin', he confiscated the very last bit o' townie contraband. He figures that if the five of them have a measly ten bullets among 'em, there'll be less temptation to stage some sort o' anti-galloway coup.

The plan is to switch off the projector in the middle of the movie and announce to the eight from the booth that they are surrounded, that they no longer have weapons, and that they are to march with hands over their heads to the one room that could double as a jail for them—namely the great big larder back at ma's. He already moved a generator and a couple of space heaters in there to make the night-cold less cruel than it proved to be for poor Henry Morganstern.

When the sound of Mel Gibson's screen voice skids into a low-pitched whine and the picture collapses into a white light on the screen, big ned lets out a blood-curdlin' *FECK IT!!* cabana springs to his feet and stares up at the projection booth. galloway, knowin' that the four men planted outside are ready to rush in with guns poised, stutters his ultimatum while John Gideon boldly swerves 'round the front row holding his two-bullet revolver in front of cabana and ned.

But cabana grabs big ned as a shield and shoves him onto Gideon— Gideon's two bullets pumpin' into ned's careenin' carcass.

trapper dan takes to bayin' like a wolf and barton pleads with galloway to let him outa this mess as they throw their arms in the air,

Western style. Far as they know there are more bullets in Gideon's gun. They look on in horror as ned's huge body gets real-white 'n shocky as he lays there shakin' and blubberin' on the floor. Swift-like Gideon slips his other friend from under his vest and begins pumpin' bullets into the others, as galloway hollers for him to stop, nearly takin' one of those bullets himself.

cabana leapfrogs over row after row of theater seats and makes it out the back door into the waitin' gun barrels of galloway's less deadly accomplices—but the four men are confused by the sheer *abundance* o' shootin' and in the confusion cabana tears off between them, leavin' two of 'em to shoot after him an' mebbe graze him. cabana is gone. The rest of the eight are shot up real bad by Gideon who uses up a good twenty bullets and puts a hole in a few sweaty foreheads before aiming his pistol straight at galloway's face.

—Don't anyone try to shoot me, y'hear! roars John Gideon. —Now, galloway, you and Halverson and Parkinson just throw down your little two-bullet specials. That's right... Now we're all gonna take a nice long walk somewhere's else. It's time for the Lord's chosen posse to run things around here.

By now Halverson is happy to part with his gun and is doin' what comes natural to him—checkin' t'see if any of the dyin' can be salvaged. Abrams and Schulberg shake their heads and leave t'go home.

The unarmed galloway walks over to look at barton, who has taken a bullet clear through the neck. His head and neck haloed in blood, he looks convincin'ly dead—more Justice John Roll than Rep-resent-ative Gabby Giffords. Not that anyone is gonna name a battle cruiser after black amos b.

galloway then walks out of the theater tellin' Gideon and the others —They're all yours! Steppin' away out of his own new order, into early re-tirement.

He can't shake the sight of a pleadin' amos b. from his mind, and as he walks off he doesn't care if John Gideon chooses to plug him from behind. He can still hear those malicious fifteen or twenty extra shots ringin' out from the theater, then hears another five or six more; he knows what that means; John Gideon is doin' a bit of mercy-killin'. Finishin' off the last seven of the eight at point-blank, beggin', squirmin' and burblin' range. Savorin' every minute of it.

visitors

Henry Morgan slouches in what has become his go-to chair, feet up on an ottoman, a cold washcloth over his forehead. There's a sharp knock followed by two short knocks at the door—the password he and Claire devised to let him know it was just her. Rose Seeton occasionally visits, as does Arlene, though during Rose's visits he'd often leave out the back way and hang out in the tunnel that led back to the center of town—what had once been a big-eight bypass, but is now just a place where you are less likely to meet up with townies. The odd rat would scamper by, sick with radiation, trippin' with curvy clawed feet on the metal seams then scurryin' off, and there was always that whistlin' sound that tunnels get that was 'specially eerie where the tunnel join'd the much wider central pipe a few hundred yards off.

Today Henry doesn't feel up to scurryin' like a frightened rat. —Come in, I'm indecent, he tells the entering Claire.

—Hi, hon. How you feeling? Arlene *and* Rose are on their way—you decide where you want to be.

—I'm not up for company, Claire. I mean, yourself excluded.

—Chest pains back?

—More like a pain in the arse. I'm sick of having to flee what has been my—er, *our* place since we first arrived in this glorified fall-out shelter.

—Listen, Henry: Arlene and Rose are frantic. Gideon is now proudly signing his name with a small letter "g"—he's closed down the bar and *left his wife*, which may mean he'll be putting the hit on sweet Miz Carla, who he now says he wants to *re-form*.

—Goddamn fundamentalists. Having high tech on your side is one thing, having God is worse. When I feel up to it, I'll give gideon a keepsake to remember amos barton by! But a troublin' image of Elvis, complete with derisive sneer, pops into his head: *better not mess with the US male...*

—Look, he says, tryin' to shake both the image and the ear-worm from his head, Arlene's worries or, God knows, Rose's or even her baby brother harold's, aren't my concern. Why in hell should I have to make myself scarce just so you can hold suffragette meetings?

—Cut the feminazi bashing, Henry. There's no way Arlene is going to sit in that tiny little room of hers all day, and she can hardly wander through the *town* now, *can* she? Carla's saloon is, as they say, CLOTHES'D. And she's at risk too. The townies—*several* of whom are now sporting, excuse me, *sportin'* small-first-letter last names—see her as somebody who *catered* to the eight.

—What about Rose? Shouldn't her head be the first to fall, now that the Revolt of the Little People is upon us?

—Yeah, but remember "ma rosemary" is one hell of a cook and bottle-washer—drygoods ingredients or no—and john gideon himself wants her to stay on and take care of *his* household needs. *You* ought to know the vacuum that develops whenever a man walks away from a good wife?

—Save the allusions, Claire. It won't get any better for you with the likes of john gideon running things. Henry reaches into a pocket of his robe for another nitro. By the way, any sightings of weird harold lately?

—Why, I thought you knew: he's in jail. Just about the only prisoner the townies have, too—with cabana escaped, and the rest of them dead.

—Is anyone thinking of coming after me, oh my sweet representative in the adult world?

—No, Halverson convinced the townies you're no threat, with your health problems and all...

—Yeah, great. Here I sit, a wuss in pyjamas with a wet washcloth for a hat. At least give me time to get back into street clothes before the Women's Book Club comes for tea.

—It's not like they don't know you're sick, Henry—don't glare at me like that. I mean, you have the right to be sick—don't you? Anyway, you decide on what you want to do, but the "ladies," as you call them, will be here shortly.

There's a knock at the back door. He decides not to hobble for the exit. He moves his chair at an angle, to face obliquely away from them as they file in. Runs the palm of his hand across two days' worth of beard growth and for once, instead of feelin' like a cowpoke off a long stay on the range, he feels the wire-brush cheek of a vagrant.

Rose and Arlene arrive together. They hug as Claire lets them in. Arlene sounds upset, but the women shut up pretty quick when Claire indicates the seated Henry facin' away from them.

How can she hug that murderous bitch?

—If this is a bad time to visit, we'll just leave and come later, Rose offers, directing her voice Henry's way.

—Suit yourself, says Henry. *Nobody here but us vegetables.*

—May I stay? Rose has the gall to ask.

Claire must know everything. Mother may I? Yes you fuckin' may, murderess.

—Suit y'self, he says, diggin' his fingers into his thighs.

—You sure? Arlene presses. —We don't want to slow down your recovery.

Million dollar word, that one. *Touché. Claire's recovery*, Henry's recovery. Might've been worse: rehab.

Henry says nothin', but Claire indicates by a nod to her visitors that her husband will hold his peace—even if he does have to listen in, the room bein' small as it is.

—Sheila Gordon can't get here, too many townies out, reports Rose Seeton.

Sheila Gordon. This little cubbyhole really is turning into Central Command for The Women's Movement. Or womankind, as john gideon likes to call it. You'd think a cunt like Rose might at least say something like I'm sorry about what happened with amos—or at least something. Ah, but I'd just shoot it down, and she knows it.

—Things look bad, continues Rose. —Our days of being able to communicate are limited. gideon is doing a "men's movement" trip: drums, higher power, the whole bit. It's just a matter of time before anyone without a moustache will either be raped or confined to barracks "for their own safety."

—What can anyone expect from a bastard like that—who took a pass on havin' kids and never got to be a kid himself? But Rose reddens, realizing what she just said. Arlene finds herself checking in with Claire, who looks away.

—They say he has no pets neither, injects Henry, but they let it slide.

The women are seated in the loveseat/sofa arrangement, around a large pot of tea Claire brewed for them. Henry declines his portion.

—Halverson's with us, and he has as many as a third of the town's men with him; Sheila Gordon is doing what she can to organize the town women and the more physically able teenagers. harold has promised to teach us how to run the ventilation equipment and the generators if we can bust him out.

—So *that's* the plan, free papa harold, start over from square one? Oh, ladies, *really...*

—I don't think so, says Rose, sippin' her tea. —He's come down a few pegs, sitting behind bars and being taunted by townies.

—Yes, and I sure was put on ice, right, MA? he blurts out reachin' discretely for a nitro.

—I'd better leave—there's no point in upsetting him; I didn't think he'd stay... She stands to leave and cannot be persuaded to give Henry more time.

The second the door closes behind Rose Seeton; Henry feels like a petulant child, a whinger. After all, hadn't *he* had the upper hand for years? She's only doing what she has to do, seizing an opportunity, and here he is whining to heaven over it instead of being a gracious loser—a real gentleman.

Arlene, his own Arlene, approaches him, as Claire follows Rose out the door to try and coax her back. She puts her smooth hand on Henry's bony shoulder and gives a little squeeze.

—Of course you hate her. But do you really think she meant for things to end up quite like this?

—I don't know. You know what they say about the road to hell...

He reaches for her and pulls her by the waist, buryin' his face in her chest. —What do you know, Arlene? How much did she tell you? He takes in her scent, a mix of stirrin' and shame.

She strokes his hair and moves her other arm around his back, taken aback by how gaunt he is.

—Henry, Henry, I'm sorry... She worries for him. —Okay, so what do I know? Let me see, she says softly. —That Claire is, in a kind of a way, my biological mother, and that you're in a kind of a way my biological father, but really, Rose has been both parents to me—and, even though "uncle" harold has never been around much, I can't let him die in a cage.

Of course. Rose would be only too happy to take revenge on him and let her own brother rot—but has to think of Arlene's feelings.

The door opens slightly, but closes again; Claire gives them time.

—How can Claire be so *able* to watch me like this? Has Rose managed to turn her against me to this extent? Just listen to me whine...

—Claire *isn't* against you. She loves you. It's just that she's off those nasty drugs, and she's been getting these hypnosis-type treatments from Doc Halverson, so she's less clingy—more independent.

—I've never seen her like this in all our years of marriage, even before this mess. What kind of treatments is he giving her?

—I'm not sure of their name, if that's what you mean... she says, still kneadin' the tense muscles of his neck and shoulders. —But she swears by them and wants us to get them too. She's also taking some kind of antidepressant, I think.

Of course. Anyone who can hang in there with an arrogant, self-absorbed bastard like me must be a depressive.

He is quietly depressed himself. Passin' on meals, sittin' up at night, starin' into space...

—And you—can you forgive me? he asks, hand over his brow as he waits, wonderin' how he could even ask, given the liberties he took, the violations.

She leans over him and cradles his head to her, lettin' him whimper for a while, near tears herself. Kisses him on the cheek and leaves as Claire discreetly enters, gives Arlene a silent wave goodbye and awaits the backlash that, with Henry, nearly always follows a moment of tenderness.

But none comes. Henry ignores her return—to take up the burnin' question of the moment: how to play out the bad hand he's been dealt.

Is there a role in the new world order for a cardiac cripple, a reformed reformer, an over-the-hill, mid-life cowboy with arteries like stiff twigs and a pathetic cravin' for tobacco...tobacco bein' the only deadly thing galloway had forbidden on his little planet—because he was "allergic," even to the sound of it bein' chawed?

Might galloway be goin' through changes? Maybe he too is comin' into touch with the kind o' feelings Henry is now drownin' in. *What are these tears but a crying in my beer, a deadly swig of that worst of all human emotions—regret.*

No, "Public Domain" would not be his last poem. He begins work on another.

Venus Betraying

The fine betrayal of you
sauntering into the bathhouse
manned by your gay friends, wearing nothing
but the black-and-white dragon kimono
I bought you.

You lie on your belly
as they lift you and expose you to the halogens
after months of letting me look
only in the dimmest light.

Two clones who are "into other men"
take turns massaging your slightly imperfect parts
—all the more delicious

writhing on the bleached wood,
half of you tensing, then the other,
then the first again,
a bored Don Juan supporting your waist
while his buddy kneads one sweet loaf at a time,
a relaxation so total that you produce,
and laugh a nervous *"pardon me..."*

"Excuse *us*," they answer,
with what fantasies?
That you're a heavy-set friend?
Who knows what they do with a woman's curves
though they adore them on the stage.

Are you adored or are you trifled?
Could you not have received
much the same attention from me?

But you were so deeply pickled in wine
whenever we made love, defending
against my interests,
the undeclared intentions...

**So now, for you, love,
this last violation
without motive.**

After he finishes it, he crumples it. *How childish. If only I could remember the better man-and-wife times. When after orgasm, she wore the butterfly rash of satisfaction on her chest, that pungent sweetness escaping the sacred vertical pout. Odd, though, turning Arlene and Rose into gay men. Claire into a fag-hag. And me, a petulant, disembodied narrator? All sad, somehow very sad.*

breakout

galloway in his cell. More an oversized tool shed, its walls dented—deformed outward in several spots from where a few rowdy townies that galloway himself salted away tried to break free. But the bolted seams managed to hold, Meccano magic, and the breakouts came to nothin' but noise and effort—effort an' noise—the thick padlock through the rings of the door and shed provin' unbreachable.

galloway slowly wakin' up, earlier than his townie guard—raisin' his arms and re-testin' the limits of his con-finement. Remembers a story Morgan told him about Black Panther leader Huey Newton—how this scrawny, tubercular, bright young man angrily spit blood at the cops when they threw him into a tiny cell. But when it finally came time to release him, he stepped free as a magnificently sculpted figure—havin' spent most of his wakin' hours doin' push-ups since there warn't any room fer any other kind of exercise. Jest push-ups. Hundreds of thousands of 'em.

All well and good for Huey Newton. He had a cause. I remember how Newton and Bobby Seale and their followers showed up at the California State Capitol carryin' guns. It made even conservative Republicans so nervous they actually pushed for more gun control in America.

galloway takes out the tiny smuggled note with *early next week —Rose* on it. Leave it to a woman to sign her name on an incriminatin' message. As though she wouldn't also be arrested if they intercepted it. *Too much into relationships, women's age-old problem, the very reason for their lack of political power...unless you call feeding all the world's babies "power"; I call it "responsibility," and I am glad to be rid of it.*

The electrical power goes on the fritz two or three times a day. *It's only a matter of time before the generators break down and they have to let me out to fix them. Better to get the back-up reactor online. Then there's the filtered air valves that feed the complex and the plants that live in the greenhouses behind the filter screens. Only I know the codes for the tamper-proof locks that prevent unauthorized equipment tampering.* gideon and the boys know that, or they would have dispatched me by now to the great beyond. *But they also know that letting me live is an invitation to future trouble, even with barton gone and Morgan out of commission. I wonder if barton ever gave Henry my note. Just a matter of time before they torture me for the code to the bunker.*

galloway receives somethin' else besides the little crumpled note pushed through the crack between the yanked-on door and the shed wall. He's been getting strange *feelin's*—intimations that someone or *somethin'* waits just outside these tin walls, tryin' to communicate. The kind of feelin' he used to get when cabana was around—after you'd done somethin' you knew he didn't like. cabana always had this way of insinuatin' his thoughts—or more usually, cab not bein' the most thoughtful o' critters—his re-ackshuns.

Now it's late Sunday night an' galloway has a strong case of the feelin's. So strong, he has to formulate his stand on bein' "rescued." Which ain't easy to do, since 1) he no longer cares what happens to him, or anybody else and 2) he's angry as hell at Rose for havin' taken the law into her own hands and takin' out his only decent conversation partner, and 3) the thought of havin' to live with cabana—likely somewhere outside the dome in a high radiation zone or somewheres inside the tunnel system—makes the prospect of dyin' seem temptin'.

If cabana does show up—like a kind of high-tech pet still loyal to its master—it'd be difficult and maybe even fatal to not go along fer the ride.

At bed-time on Sunday, galloway is let out of the tin shed to have his nighttime stretch and take a leak—even gideon won't keep a man holed up with his own piss in a five-by-eight with nothin' but a slat fo' a window. John Gomez, an unremarkable townie, escorts him to a little niche in the pipes he calls his *office*—complete with a picture of his wife and two kids—and tries as usual to make conversation—keepin' his revolver 'cross his lap for future reference. Course John who'd worked as a fitter and welder could easily handle the likes of galloway with one hand tied behind his back.

—Mr. Galloway—er—Harold, are you willin' yet to give mister gideon the combination to your bunker—so he can get at the master plans and instructions? Sorry to keep askin' you, but I was told to keep at it.

"Harold" indeed. *Where does this insolent joe-average townie get off...*

I know what gideon wants. The lap of luxury pulls on fundamentalists as hard as it does on non-believers.

—Ignore me again, huh? Well...suit yerself. It's just that if I were you, my back and joints would be pretty stiff from sittin' in a cage, day after day. I'd want out... Maybe put in for a transfer to the larder, where there's more room.

—What's to stop your boss from killing me once he gets what he wants? asks galloway blandly, his tone changin' because against the metal pipe ahead of him is an equally metallic shadow of a half-clothed form about three-quarters the size cabana used to be. In a second John Gomez catches galloway's eyes doin' a dart an' he swerves around to see what's behind him, but cabana turns his face too—his body blendin' with the side of the pipe and no longer detectable.

Gomez turns back to galloway real-quick as if expectin' to have been jumped by now: —Why, you connivin'? says Gomez, reachin' for his gun and slowly risin' from his chair. —Tryin' to fake me out?

But a python slinks around Gomez's neck and a second springin' snake plucks his gun and throws it to harold galloway who simply looks down at it with a disinterest'd look. The coil tightens 'til Gomez's eyes start to bulge and a gurgle comes from his broken windpipe, as he looks 'round for the picture of his wife and kids, on the verge of becomin' history. cabana lets him fall to the ground in a swoon, then picks up the thrown gun himself, lookin' through his reluctant escapee, and holds the gat face-even with the squirmin' Gomez.

—Please! Please! Don't shoot! wheezes Gomez, doin' a feeble break-dance, arms 'n legs twitchin' as he looks straight into cabana's bloodshot agates. In a second galloway steps between cab and Gomez, tryin' to hustle the disabled guard into the tin shed. Gomez trips over his own feet and stumbles into the tiny space as two shots pop neatly through harold galloway's white-shirted back.

cabana reaches into the shed, screams ringin' in the tight space—and in the gadawfullest loud noise that ever rung out in a confine, John Gomez is shot straight through, the bullet ricochetin' an' nabbin' cabana's right arm.

Lookin' pissed off even fo' him, cabana lopes away, his gun hand holdin' his bloodied right arm—the daze of havin' shot his maker slowly dawnin'.

bad news

Henry awakens from his daily afternoon nap—two or three hours at a stretch some afternoons—a nap that leaves him wide-eyed and unable to sleep at night.

News from Sheila Gordon, who rushes over with Arlene, the two of them frantic about bein' unable to reach Rose. —He's dead! harold is dead. And the combinations and master plans gone with him.

Henry don't budge, just pulls the cover of his cot over his ear and listens.

—He must have tried to escape, because he was shot through the back—by his guard, Anita Gomez's husband John.

Morgan can't see his old "friend" Zwyxy taking a risk like that. galloway warn't cut out for great escapes... But he jest lies there and savors his right to stay out of it.

—Somehow, harold managed to also kill Gomez—with Gomez's own gun.

What? A shot-from-behind galloway wrestlin' away the gun of a powerful guard? Or what? galloway gettin' hold of Gomez's gun, shootin' him, but somehow losin' the gun to a strugglin' Gomez who still has enough power left to pump him twice? Fancy-full scenarios.

—As for Gomez, his poor wife couldn't even identify him, because he was shot up close through the face.

Henry Morgan swings his legs round. Stands up bare-chested and in blue jeans, startlin' the three good women. —Only one thing kills like that.

Claire mouths the *c*-word.

The others nod. Henry Morgan rises, splashes water on his face near the little sink and mirror, straps on his droopy gun belt and walks out the front exit of the little apartment for the first time since he'd been brought there from the infirmary. Claire don't call *Wait!* after him—she jest sits down with Arlene and Sheila Gordon beside her, each of them shakin' their heads and wonderin' if the last of the big eight is set to ride again.

But Henry is back in a minute. Walks right by them to his bedstand to open a bottle, countin' out eight or nine nitros into a little aspirin tin that he slides into the back pocket of his jeans. —Extra rounds, he winks as he tramps out a whole lot slower than he used to, but standin' straight for the first time since he lost his battle with ma's ungodly deep-freeze.

in search of cabana

The key is to find cabana before meetin' up with john gideon and his men. If he's to resonate with the vibes cabana puts out, he had best clear his mind—though he might also have to talk john gideon out of killin' him.

He has a hunch cabana will revisit galloway's bunker, around the same place he—as the once-mighty henry—used to lie in wait for galloway—the very spot where galloway would be if he were still runnin' the show. But there are few hidin' places near that part of the dome and no way of gettin' through those thick steel trapdoors that hold the remains of the old civilization—if'n you lack the proper com-bine-ation.

It's crazy to be out here. gideon's likely sent a few men to comb the settlement for cabana—but the head of Henry Morgan might do fine in a pinch. gideon likely figures cab would leave the sealed portion of the complex to risk the radiation outside—the way big ned often did.

What's more: if Henry is spotted by a townie and the word gets out that he's gettin' 'round again, there might be rumors that he, and not cabana, had tried to free galloway—with *the two of them* killin' John Gomez in the process. But it's only several hundred yards of pipe and then a brief walk at ground level to get to galloway's bunker, and he figures he c'n manage it—if he pops a nitro every couple hundred yards.

He lies on the ground alongside a pipe seam, recovers his strength, and ever so quietly tunes in—for cabana.

encounter

But Henry can't reach galloway's bunker—and it ain't his heart, but his legs that stop him cold. Shootin' pains up his calves—both of them—ya c'n only walk so far on legs that have been idle for days. He's been back to "rollin' pills"—homemade ciggies—dippin' back into the stash ole harold galloway laid on him after galloway himself quit, "for vaping only," and this return to the old habit, while it helps his mood, don't help his legs none. So he's forced to take a nitro and jest stand and rest a while—which makes him a target for both former friend and foe.

By the time he reaches the heavy steel door—three nitros later—he feels whoozy, near to passin' out. Pourin' sweat and wishin' he had put on more than just a shirt and vest, his teeth begin to chatter. Memories of ma's larder.

And there, about a hundred yards ahead of him, looking live as fresh bait, is Rose. He c'n see her walkin' slowly towards him and he knows that if he's gonna repay his "debt" to her in full, this is his chance. She too is carryin' some kind of piece—a small pistol affair he can't identify at this range. Is she out huntin' too?

—Henry! she calls. —What're you *doing* out here...

—Catchin' my death, he calls back—then feels his legs shake 'n go rubbery as he collapses in a heap jest outside galloway's bunker, his head narrowly missin' the metal trapdoor. When he comes to—he still feels clammy, but not as weak an' his head is in Rose's lap. She and Arlene, who is also wearin' a gun on a makeshift kind of belt-holster—had somehow walked, dragged or carried him back to Claire's.

Women with guns. Wet dream of Wayne LaPierre.

deposition

They lay Henry's failin' body across a cot at Claire's. Rose draws a basinful of warm water and drops a hand towel into it while Arlene pulls a sheet borrowed from the hospital up over his shiverin' form. He remains silent—except for once mutterin' *What's the use*—as he looks up at the concerned faces of the women millin' about him.

As she sets water on to boil, Rose remembers somethin'. Somethin' she'd noticed as the women hauled a gaunt but deadweight Henry back to the apartment. The out-the-corner-of-one-eye apparition happened about forty or fifty yards down the pipe—somethin' shaped like a vat. But with a hat. A vat with a hat. She did a double-take then, but with the weight of half of Henry Morgan to support, didn't dare bring it to Arlene's attention. It was as if somethin' wouldn't let her *do* that.

—I saw *him*! *It*! she stammers to Arlene and Claire. —cabana's out there! And before the others c'n even react, there's a dull dead thud of a knock on the door, like a dead fist landin'.

—Make like Henry's dead! she tells the others. —Don't ask—just do it! Battle stations...

—One moment, honey, darlin', Rose drawls sweetly, wavin' Claire away, but instead of headin' for the door, she heads for the cupboard—sweepin' a bottle of ketchup and squirtin' a big blob of it into her basin of water. In the same motion she throws the mess of it on the covers over Henry and pulls the drippy sheet over his face. Arlene and Claire stand back in a frozen posture. The door strains at its hinges and comes crashin' to the floor, narrowly missin' Arlene's foot. Fillin' the emptied doorway is cabana—his huge gray arms streaked with dried blood—with the eyes of a bewildered desert animal.

A menacin' grin spreads across his face as Miz Cahluh begins to wail, indicatin' the bloody sheet over Henry's body: —Dead, cab, Henry's dead!! And john gideon says yo're next!! Yo're the last of the eight, cab!

cabana jest smiles out from under his sweat—licks a canine and moves forward to inspect the cadaver of his former rival. He registers a long pale arm hanging limp from the bed. And a whole mess o' red.

Rose throws her arms around his granite shoulders and puts her cheek to his slate face: he backs up a might, his face recoilin' an' his arms takin' up the blockin' stance of a samurai. He lifts the huge door while the women look on in terror—he's lookin' like he might just heave it at the remains of Morgan—but then sets it down at an angle in the doorway, backs slowly out into the tunnel—and is gone.

Rose sits down on a chair as Arlene and Claire each place a hand on her back—drained and relieved.

—amos used to say that chocolate sauce made great blood in the days of black-and-white films, says Rose.

—I could go for some of that, says a thin voice from under the covers, startlin' the women, who don't know whether to laugh or cry. —Ah'm beginnin' t'feel like a freedom fry.

Shots ring out and four hearts are pounding.

Rose hadn't been the only one to spot cabana earlier. gideon's men were on his trail, and were there to welcome him at the exit to the tunnel system.

a deal

When john gideon and his men step through the empty doorway of Claire's apartment with smokin' guns drawn, they nearly back out at the sight of a ghostly white Henry Morgan sittin' up on his cot with a bloodied sheet around his waist. The men fill the room with their autumn bulkiness, as the women circle around Morgan as if to protect him.

Says Henry to gideon: —I still walk the land of the living... albeit with a little help from my friends.

The *al-be-it* is in response to gideon's outfit. gideon wears a bulky tweed overcoat with a blue blazer, a black sweater, and a white dress shirt worn backwards under it all—to give the effect of a preacher's collar. His thinnin' hair is slicked back with some kind of gel. Morgan is surprised that none of gideon's men look like they're in drug withdrawal; instead they seem hopped up, energetic—*game*.

gideon must have coaxed out of galloway the locations of the drug caches outside galloway's personal bunker. Might even have managed to obtain access to the bunker itself. If *that* is true, then what did he and Rose and Arlene and Claire—or The Girls, as he's begun to think of this new gang of four—have left to bargain with? A sheet full of numbers...

The preacher pulls up an empty chair, turns it to face him, and straddles it. —Well, Morgan, you look depleted—but not *too* grave, given the apparent blood loss. Sniffs the stale room air. —What're you guys doin'—a ketchup commercial? His men snicker and laugh and the women try to look amused. They know to keep still when gideon holds court.

—Well, Morgan, we have your pal cabana on the run.

—Sounded like you got him pretty good. Ambush-style.

—Well, we keep grazin' him, but he don't go down easy. Not like the next-to-last member of the eight.

—galloway's dead, says Morgan.

—We can't claim credit for that one.

—Show a little heart, mr. christian revival. This woman here happens to be his *sister*, says an exhausted Henry.

—Listen, con-valescent, *my* heart's not nearly as bleedin' as yours. As for these collaboratin' harridans, they'll be lucky if they find grace with me and manage to stay alive.

He continues: —Now you women had best go and look after preparin' some meals for my men. As of today, Claire and Arlene, you will remain with me *to look after my personal needs*. Rose will attend to the needs of my household. He looks Arlene up and down as he says this.

—No, says Henry Morgan, my wife stays here, and Arlene—who's actually like my own *daughter*—goes on living by herself, as she has been doing.

gideon grins. —Ain't *three* women a bit rich for a soft-shell-crab senior like yourself?

—Let's cut a deal, gideon. A deal involving the women too. Claire and Rose and Arlene exchange looks—surprised as gideon is, even as Henry is, to hear him speak with any of the old authority.

—It'll be an exchange. A disarmament by you and your men, and the settin' up of an election—with women's votes countin' the same as men's.

gideon laughs. —And I presume that *cabana* will also throw down his guns and come in on this little *deal*?

—I thought about that. We'll allow your men, and whatever town faction that opposes you, to hang on to a couple of guns each side—let the community keep a look-out for cabana. The right to a well regulated militia, and all that... But we don't need more than a couple of guns each side. Henry realizes as he says this that a recent effort to limit gideon to two bullets in a single gun hadn't fared too well.

—You really want to turn back the clock, don't you Henry? To the days of disarmament treaties and "Mutual Assured Destruction" and all that garbage; as if it worked *then*. As if it could work. Oh, yesss, we have two rifles and they have two rifles—so that jest about ought to keep us out of each other's hair—right? Bullshit! At least galloway had the good sense to know that the only way to run a society is to keep things *hoppin'*—keep everyone too busy or too scared to ponder all the "Big Questions," which only cause them to band together in idealistic *movements* up to no good: the ecology *movement*, the civil rights *movement*, the women's *movement*, the occupy *movement*—anythin' just to evade our core christian values.

—If you don't like "movements," why dress up as a preacher? The voice is Arlene's. Henry signals her to shut up.

john gideon pulls his gun and slowly aims it in an arc at each of Arlene's breasts. He cocks the trigger, then aims towards the ground, firin' a shot just shy of her foot. She flinches and cries out. He continues: —You're a mite too pretty to kill, Miss Cahluh, but we do ask you to bottle up your cleverness—the way you once did. You keep on purrin'...

Henry flinches worse than Arlene and asks Claire to hand him some of those nitros, which gideon allows...

—Another thing galloway knew, says gideon, was how to keep everybody *happy*, and ever since he's been dead there's a lot of us here in town that are a mite *irritable*, havin' to take on the world with nothin' but booze for a cushion. Me and my boys here have decided that the power of faith does as well as booze—but some of my townie deputies do miss the manna pappy harold made fall from heaven.

—Well, gideon, I can help. I'll provide the combination to galloway's bunker and lessons in some of his surveillance equipment that I picked up during my visits to the bunker. That'll go a ways to helpin' you deal with the cabana problem... You guys get the run of what little is left of "the good life" around here—in exchange for some general peace and lettin' folks work out a way of tryin' to be happy enough under strained conditions.

—'Til the food runs out? jeers gideon. —We plan to ration some of these townie mutations—if only to extend the food supply as long as we can. What does happen when we run out of food?

—Then it's time to test the limits of life outside the complex. But we need to do it as one people—men and women together, able-bodied or not.

—All Children of Israel, nods gideon. —And this "disarmament" of yours—who's going to carry it out, the UN? He laughs and his men uneasily join in.

—galloway kept a strict count of existin' weapons including those that ended up in the hands of townies and "unauthorized big eight candidates." So, I think if we had a great big pile of guns turned in we'd be able to figure out which ones were still missin'—start conductin' searches and announce that no drugs and no other goodies will be given out to anybody 'til *every* gun is turned in.

As he talks, Henry Morgan's hands and arms begin to pink up. Rose indicates this to Claire, who finds herself again drawn to the grayin' eminence now negotiatin' with gideon. An agin' calm and confidence have replaced the old empty swagger. He may have little control over his life, but he has a renewed sense of how to tap the power of others.

—You know, Morgan, I reckon me and my boys could *induce* you to hand over some of this special knowledge you have, *without* having to sell the farm to get it...

—What're you talkin', gideon? Torture...? You look at this face of mine. I reckon I've finally earned the title *white man*. You *really* think torture will work, on a ticker like mine? Besides, you start torturin' folks, you lose legitimacy. I don't know that Doc Halverson will work for torturers.

—What's he got that you ain't got? taunts gideon. As fer these "free elections" you want, Morgan—you wouldn't be thinkin' o' runnin' in them, now would you?

—I have no such intention. Maybe Rose Seeton would like to, though.

She pampered the eight, but only in an effort to contain them. Did her brother a real favor. I reckon we all owe her somethin' for that. Anyway, gideon, I'm pretty sure that you would get most of the town's votes—if only 'cause you've always been the biggest and strongest and, 'cept for Halverson, the smartest of the townsfolk. But let's scale down the power thing some. Let's not just do another harold galloway.

—How about I go along with the disarmament *and* the elections—it's the great American way—but not the women votin' idea...which is not how I interpret Scripture.

—What do you have against the women, gideon? You afraid we might organize against you? challenges Rose.

gideon's boys have a hoot over this, and one of them slaps his boss and says —Shucks, john, you're just worried that if you can't lord it over the women then none of them are gonna sleep with you. And all four of the guys take to laughin' and gideon with them and the three women come pretty close to joinin' on that one.

—Well, I'm feelin' a might weak, says Henry. —What say we adjourn for now; you, gideon, let Claire and Arlene stay with me, and escort Rose home—I'm sure you're still willin' to make our new friend mister gideon his evenin' meal, aren't you Rose? By tomorrow you can decide on the changes I'm proposin'.

—Tell you what, Morgan. We start afresh, and we do things right. Just like old times, in good old GOP America. But if we set up a republic here then you become its first prisoner. I'll hose down that little tin room where galloway ex-pired.

—*No!* from Claire and Arlene.

—You and Rose Seeton. We'll pardon the pretty young thing and the pretty not-so-young thing. Oh...and you oldsters will make do with separate cells, he grins.

Just then Morgan has an image—of a kid from his past who regularly showed up in his nightmares, a squat muscular bully named Darren "Gator" Gates. Darren used to love pickin' out another kid, *selectin'* him, then informin' him that he was goin' to *really* cause him pain. The kid, picked for no reason, would sometimes try to wriggle off the hook—maybe say to Darren: —Aren't you related to Micah Gates, down the street? I *know* him... But Darren would smile and say —That all depends why you're askin'. If it's to try and get me to give up my plan, then I ain't gonna answer you... If you're just tryin' to make conversation *even though you accept my punishment*, then I'll say —Sure, he's my cousin... At that point the victim would spot in Gates's eyes the pure unmitigated delight of the bully.

Which is what Henry figures he spots in gideon's glistenin' irises. The little smilin' crow's feet aroun' his eyes. Henry looks to Rose, who looks to gideon and his four heavily armed stalwarts and returns a *What's the use* look. Henry nods his acceptance.

—But all safeguards have to be in place before I give up any of what I know. Besides, the power could fail at any time...

gideon waxes magnanimous: —I shall commute ma's sentence and have her do Alternate Measures in the form of the cleanin' and culinary arts she's so good at. But you Morgan—you're gonna do time as the next-to-last survivin' member of the eight, not just as a museum piece but as bait for to lure the shark we still have circlin' us.

Henry flinches at gideon's take on the big eight accent. But bites his lip.

—Okay, says Henry, but do I have your word—in front of these four men—on a free vote, with the women takin' part?

—My word in the eyes of God *and* in the eyes of my men. So long as we're left with enough firepower to deal with cabana *and* we get the run of galloway's defense network *and* you're willing to pay a rightful price for your complicity in the Old Way of doing things, *then* we can have a fair election.

—An election where both men and *women* vote?

gideon looks at his men. They just shrug. The *search me...* sign.

gideon nods.

Henry recalls that gideon was one of the dozen tradesmen, guys with only high school education at best, that galloway risked taking into the new arrangement. Maybe they would develop an interest in a little civics, given enough time.

—Who do you want to rep-resent you on the committee to draw all this up, while you're in the slammer? How 'bout Doc Halverson?

—Henry's eyes dart towards Rose, Arlene...Claire.

—Halverson, yes—Sheila Gordon too.

john gideon smiles as his men, with tips of their Stetson hats, file out. *Exeunt.*

—There are still a couple items, says gideon, afore he leaves the frame.

—First: we need a chronicler of these End Times. I found a thick pile of notes left behind by galloway's lawyer, that "Slim" guy, Reggie Canuck. Smart-ass Canadjyun—real smart-ass David Frum type.

—Isn't that his to keep writin'?

—He got caught in a crossfire, two weeks past.

—God. So, what polio couldn't do...

—Yup. I even have his guitar, and yo're welcome to it. But how about you take it on? You'll have plenty o' down time ahead o' you, solitary time, and you always were one for writin' things.

Stunned by the news about Reggie, Henry asks —What do you want me to call it, *gideon's bible*?

—Call it whatever you want. Call it *The Book of cabana*, for all I care. But we have a final item o' business: I got me a piece of meat at home in the ice box. Kind of a leg o' lamb. Sacrificial lamb. I went back to fetch it from a rooftop—lost sleep over it, you might say. I expect you to eat it once it thaws. I'll cook it up real nice fo' you—Hannibal Lecter-style—now there's a godless book I bet you read.

gideon grows more peaceful. Yet he can't pass up a partin' shot: —And when you're finally dead, Morgan*stern*, and have one last chance to rise again, the angel Gabriel's gonna shake his golden locks and ask —You looked at *HOW MANY* sets of genitals?

The moment gideon and his men leave with Rose Seeton followin' in tow—sulkin' along after them—Arlene and Claire give Henry a kiss, each too exhausted to debate with him the wisdom of makin' any sort o' deal with the likes of john gideon.

Henry knows whose leg he'll be pickin' at. A voice inside whispers *Just desserts.*

Henry folds the sheet around himself, which still reeks of ketchup, lies back down on his side and sinks into the deepest sleep he's had since he first came in under the dome of harold galloway and associates.

The End

Acknowledgements

Thanks to close friends and cousins for early, frank discussions about the largely unexplored relationship between guns and male adequacy. The late Eugene "Gene" Hluschak and Paul Teskey helped me understand these relationships, and I first heard the amusing taunt, "Excuse me, sir, but is that your *gun?*" from Paul. That was more than forty-five years ago.

Thanks to the Canadian authors of *Enter the Babylon System: Unpacking Gun Culture from Samuel Colt to 50 Cent*, Rodrigo Bascunan and Christian Pearce, and to American social activist Geoffrey Canada for his revelatory, autobiographical book, *Fist, Stick, Knife, Gun*, which helped me consolidate early conceptions of the role guns play in shoring up male adequacy. *Albion's Seed*, by David Hackett Fischer, taught me about the influence of two groups of English immigrants to the United States, groups that settled Virginia and Appalachia, whose folkways contributed to a culture of great music, but also to patriarchy, misogyny, the adulation of weapons and the corporal punishment of children. These "borderer"

Southern accents are used by Slim Reggie, especially when he speaks in an outrageously frank voice.

Many thanks for the encouragement received by friends and editors who poured or plodded through earlier versions of the manuscript and offered constructive criticism at various stages of the book's development, including Len Leven, Mike McCabe for putting in some early sweat equity, and my longtime associate Wayde. Alana Wilcox was the first female reader to praise the book, at a critical juncture. Thanks to Jon Ennis, who put up with me endlessly referring to a book that he is finally getting to read.

Special thanks to Deanna Janovski for helping me stay true to my new linguistic rules while recommending I break them, now and then, to keep the reader on board, to David Jang for his evocative book design, and to Heather Wood and Jeff Kirby for their work at the managerial and promotional ends of the enterprise.

The cover photo is by the inimitable iPhone photographer DraMan, aka Roger Guetta. Author photo by Rebecca Gilgan.

All poems in the book, with the exception of "A Correct Compassion" by James Kirkup, were written by the author in his other identity. The five stanzas of the long poem "A Correct Compassion" are quoted with permission from The James Kirkup Collection. Sophie Glazer first alerted me to the poem.

On page 135, the quote "I didn't take the goddamn fish out of the ocean" evokes the words of former Canadian federal Minister of Fisheries and Oceans, John Crosbie of Newfoundland.

On page 151 there is a paragraph laced with a number of invented words by Anthony Burgess, from his visionary dystopian novel, *A Clockwork Orange*.

I borrow some descriptions from Canadian physician poet Vincent Hanlon's poem "Sleep Deprivation," which appeared in my poetry anthology, *The Naked Physician*.

This is a work of fiction. While the author uses the self in disparate ways and several of the poems are written in a confessional mode, it is not autobiographical. No character is identical to any person, living or dead.

Special thanks to author Terry Fallis for providing back cover commentary that helped me appreciate the complexity of my narrator, and to Jim Nason and the team at Tightrope for having the guts to publish this book and not fret over any untoward reactions.

As always, I thank my wonderful wife and children for respecting my need for a free-range imagination.

Other Books by Ron Charach

POETRY

The Big Life Painting

The Naked Physician

Someone Else's Memoirs

Past Wildflowers

Petrushkin!

Dungenessque

Elephant Street

Selected Portraits

Forgetting the Holocaust

ESSAYS

Cowboys and Bleeding Hearts

About the author

Ron Charach is a Toronto psychiatrist and the author of nine collections of poetry, most recently *Selected Portraits* (2007) and *Forgetting the Holocaust* (2011). His poems and essays have appeared in most Canadian literary and medical/psychiatric journals.